Hell Bound

Hellscourge: Book 3

J.C. DIEM

Copyright © 2016 J.C. DIEM

All rights reserved. Published by Seize The Night Agency.

No part of this publication may be reproduced or transmitted in any form or by any means, electronic or mechanical, including photocopying, recording, storage in an information retrieval system, or otherwise, without the prior written permission of the author.

ISBN-13: 978-1533691507
ISBN-10: 1533691509

This is a work of fiction. Names, characters, places, incidents and dialogues are products of the author's imagination or are used fictitiously. Any resemblance to actual people, living or dead, events or locales is entirely coincidental.

Cover by: Ravven

www.ravven.com

Cover Photograph (female model) Copyright © 2016 by J.C. Diem

Titles by J.C. Diem:

Mortis Series
Death Beckons
Death Embraces
Death Deceives
Death Devours
Death Betrays
Death Banishes
Death Returns
Death Conquers
Death Reigns

Shifter Squad Series
Seven Psychics
Zombie King
Dark Coven
Rogue Wolf
Corpse Thieves
Snake Charmer
Vampire Matriarch
Web Master
Hell Spawn

Hellscourge Series
Road To Hell
To Hell And Back
Hell Bound
Hell Bent
Hell To Pay
Hell Freezes Over
Hell Raiser
Hell Hath No Fury
All Hell Breaks Loose

Fate's Warriors Trilogy
God Of Mischief
God Of Mayhem
God Of Malice

Loki's Exile Series
Exiled
Outcast
Forsaken
Destined

Hunter Elite Series
Hunting The Past
Hunting The Truth
Hunting A Master
Hunting For Death
Hunting A Thief
Hunting A Necromancer
Hunting A Relic
Hunting The Dark
Hunting A Dragon

Half Fae Hunter Series
Dark Moon Rising
Deadly Seduction
Dungeon Trials
Dragon Pledge

Unseelie Queen

Chapter One

Pristine white snow drifted lazily from the overcast sky. It was beautiful until the moment it hit the sidewalk. Then it turned into an ugly gray slush, which fit in perfectly with my current mood.

The entire city of Manhattan was gray at the moment, both in color and in atmosphere. It was the middle of January and the weather had recently taken a turn for the worse. I'd lived in Denver my whole life and winter could sometimes be pretty harsh there. The few inches of snow that had fallen during the past couple of hours didn't impress me much. They'd predicted that a storm would hit us sometime soon, but it hadn't made an appearance yet.

My contemplation of the dismal sky was interrupted when Brie spoke. "You need to pay more attention to your surroundings." Her tone was shrill and scolding and frankly made me want to strangle her. "Are you even listening to me?" she said sharply when I made no effort to respond to her.

"Nope." I'd learned that honesty was the best policy when I dealt with her. Being blunt to the point of rudeness also had the bonus of getting on her nerves. "I'm thinking about the weather in an effort to drown out your incessant nagging."

Pressing her lips together tightly, she glared at me as she tried to get her temper under control. We had a truce to try not to stab each other, but we would never be the best of friends. Our personalities were too similar to make that possible. We were both too sarcastic and snarky for our own good.

"I am trying to assist you," she said with exaggerated patience. "How will you ever learn to be the warrior that this world needs if you refuse to listen to me?" Like me, she wore a long black coat. The weather didn't bother angels, but they had to at least try to blend in with the human populace. Her curly blond hair was short and never needed to be cut. Once a celestial being took possession of a vessel, their body stopped changing. Unfortunately for her, she'd chosen a fourteen-year-old girl to inhabit. She looked young, but was actually millions or maybe even billions of years old. Her superior attitude had grated on me from the first day that we'd met. It hadn't become any less annoying with time.

I rolled my eyes and started to walk away. She grabbed my arm and turned me towards her. "The least you can do is acknowledge me when I speak to you." Her tone was tightly controlled. It was a sure sign that she was going to lose her patience soon.

"I rolled my eyes, didn't I?" I said with my usual sarcasm and yanked my arm free. "How much more acknowledgement do you need from me?" She took a deep breath, which I knew was a prelude to an explosion. I spoke again before she could unleash her temper on me. "Let me explain something to you, since we're obviously having severe communication issues. It isn't what you say that makes me want to ignore you. It's the way you say it that drives me nuts."

As I'd hoped, her explosion was diverted. I really wasn't in the mood to suffer through one of her angry tirades. Sniffing in annoyance, she crossed her arms. "You are being ridiculous."

"This is what you just sounded like," I said. I copied her posture and parroted her words back at her, using the same snarky tone, but at a much higher pitch.

Eyes narrowing in affront, she drew herself up to her full height, which was a couple of inches shorter than my five-foot-five. "Well then, since you apparently do not approve of the methods I use, I will take my leave of you." Her eyes gleamed and she grinned slyly, as if she knew something that I didn't. "It will be interesting to see how well you do without my guidance."

She teleported herself away, leaving me standing on

the sidewalk alone. "Snotty little cow," I muttered beneath my breath. I hated the fact that the angels could zap themselves away whenever we were in the middle of an argument. They had many talents that I lacked, but teleportation was the coolest of them all.

It was rare for me to be alone and I savored the silence. One of my friends, or allies in Brie's case, was always nearby. As the scourge of hell, I was the best and only hope the world had of avoiding a demon apocalypse. Being human, I could enter and leave hell at will. Three of our team members were angels, which meant they couldn't even set foot in the shadowlands. Leo had tried it once and had quickly become ill. He hadn't even made it halfway along the passage that led to the misty lands that separated Earth from hell before he'd had to turn back. Sam was an imp, so he could also come and go when needed. He'd become a member of my entourage, which meant I could take him along with me whenever I was bound for the underworld. Sophia wasn't an angel anymore and could probably go with us. But she was more of a scholar than a warrior.

Speaking of lack of fighting skills, I'd started out this endeavor without any combat experience whatsoever. My friends were doing their best to train me during our down time. We had a lot of free time on our hands, so my fighting skills were slowly being honed.

A month had passed since Sam and I had entered the eighth realm of hell and had returned with our prize. I now had two of the strange metal pieces. Once I'd found all nine pieces, they could supposedly be joined together to create an object of power.

Since we'd returned, I hadn't received any new clues about how to get to the seventh realm of hell. We were killing time until I found the next portal that would take us to the shadowlands. This included going out on patrols around the city. We weren't just searching for the next entrance to hell, we were also looking for demons. They seemed to have gone into hiding lately. We were trying to locate them so we could entice them into traps and whittle down their numbers. It was also excellent hands-on combat training for me.

There were two downsides to this plan. The first was that I absorbed the demon souls that were evicted from their host, adding to the legion that were inside me. The second was that innocent humans died every time we ejected their evil hijackers. If there was another way to get the hell spawn out of their hosts, I hadn't found it yet. Leo had watched an old movie about exorcism with Sam and me a couple of weeks ago. He'd laughed so hard that he'd fallen off the couch. Apparently, demons couldn't be forced out through holy water and stern prayer.

It had been Brie's turn to escort me on patrol this time. Now that she'd abandoned me, I would have to perform a search of the area on my own. She'd teleported us to Stuyvesant Town, according to a sign that we'd passed earlier. It was an area that I wasn't familiar with. Despite all of the patrols that I'd been on, there were still entire neighborhoods that I hadn't seen yet.

Gigantic apartment buildings loomed beside me. They were made of brick and were identical, or very close to it. I could see the East River a short distance away. A freeway curved upwards, ruining what would have been a pleasant view. An incessant flood of cars drove along it, bringing the inevitable noise and air pollution with them.

Few people were out on foot. There had been a lot of murders in the city since I'd arrived here three months ago. Most people were afraid to walk the streets now. Fewer tourists were braving the city because of the deaths. The Christmas season had been dismal for most stores.

It wasn't just the seemingly random killings that was causing fear to run high. The bodies of over a dozen pretty blond teenage girls had been discovered. All bore at least a superficial resemblance to me. Their hearts had been removed, either in a fit of rage that the victims weren't me, or for the sheer pleasure of causing them pain.

The police were beginning to suspect that the murders of the girls were linked to the other bodies that had been found scattered around the city. They were right, of course. Demons were behind most of the stabbings, but we were responsible for some of the deaths. We were better at hiding the bodies, yet some of them had probably been discovered by now.

We'd been confused when the demons had suddenly started being evicted from their hosts. We'd come to the conclusion that rival bands of hell spawn were deliberately killing each other's vessels. They knew that their souls would be drawn to me. It was an expedient way of ridding themselves of their competition.

No matter who was responsible for the murders, all of the deaths were due to the war that was raging between demons and angels. It was apparently my task to put an end to the conflict. Manhattan might be small compared to other cities, but it was packed with people. Everyone was vulnerable to being possessed either by a demon or an angel. I was apparently the only one who couldn't be taken over. My missing soul was to blame, or maybe to thank, for that. I didn't have to worry that a demon would take control of me and turn me to the dark side.

With an internal sigh, I brought my focus back to the task at hand. Brie and I had already walked around the perimeter of Stuyvesant Town without seeing anything of interest. I was tempted to head back to our base, but that was probably what she expected me to do. Figuring she was probably watching me from somewhere close by, I didn't want to give her the satisfaction of seeing me give up on my mission.

Turning towards a flight of stairs that led deeper into the brick buildings, I began to climb. My head whipped towards a scraggly tree when I caught a flutter of something black from the corner of my eye. Winter had stolen the leaves away, leaving the trees bare and vulnerable. My hand flew to the dagger that was hidden inside a pocket of my coat. My tension eased when I saw it wasn't the undead raven. It was just an errant plastic bag that had become caught on a branch.

Resuming my climb, I was watching my feet when I saw the shadow of a bird soar past. I looked up to see a lone pigeon landing in one of the trees that lined the staircase. It turned its head sideways and seemed to be staring straight at me.

Tripping on the next step, I caught myself on the railing and watched where I was walking as I climbed. The raven had spooked me so badly during our previous encounters that I jumped whenever I saw anything with wings.

Telling myself to stop acting like a scared little girl, I glanced up again and froze. In the few seconds that I'd been distracted, more birds had arrived. Dozens of them now crowded the branches and I hadn't even heard them gather. There were sparrows, seagulls, blue jays, woodpeckers, ducks and even a few pelicans. There were more that I didn't recognize. Crows were among the throng as well. They stared at me malevolently, reminding me far too much of the bird that had been stalking me for months.

Hearing a familiar mocking caw, I searched the area until I found the creature that I'd been dreading. The skeletal raven perched on a windowsill on the third floor of an apartment building. Its feathers were dull rather than glossy and bone showed through in a few places. It had presumably been taken to hell while alive to become the eyes and ears of the current Hellmaster. Over time, it had turned into an unholy creature that was neither dead, nor alive. Like all creatures that resided in the underworld, it was imbued with evil.

Its single milky eye watched me slyly as I began to back away. I'd sliced the other one out in an attempt to fend it off when it had attacked me. I was pretty sure it was still seeking revenge for the wound that I'd inflicted on it. Black blood still oozed sluggishly from the empty socket. It didn't look like the injury was ever going to heal.

The other birds turned to keep me in view as I continued to back down the stairs. I gripped the railing so I wouldn't fall and crack my head open on the cement. My heart was thudding hard as I neared the bottom step. The raven opened its beak and I whirled around and took off at a sprint. It uttered a harsh croak, which was the signal for the flock to attack.

Chapter Two

Wings fluttered loudly, drowning out the sounds of traffic as the birds obeyed their undead leader. One of them hit me in the back and I stumbled forwards. I flicked a look over my shoulder to see a seagull lying on the sidewalk in a daze. It shook its head and stumbled to its feet, then prepared to launch itself into the air again.

Sparrows and other small birds darted around me. Fast and nimble, they were going for my eyes. I covered my face with my hands. It wasn't easy to run while half blind, but I managed it without tripping over. The few pedestrians who were out and about screamed and ran when they saw the milling mass of birds that were dive bombing me.

Beaks pecked at my face and hands mercilessly. Talons became tangled in my hair as I was chased down the sidewalk. The noise of the chirps and shrieks was a horrible cacophony that would be sure to give me nightmares. Even above the racket, I could hear the raven cawing in what sounded like laughter.

Tearing the birds out of my hair, I batted them away with my hands to give myself a short reprieve. I desperately searched for a way to escape from them. A small delivery truck parked on the side of the road up ahead caught my eye. The delivery driver stepped outside the small grocery store and saw the incoming birds. He wisely leaped back inside and slammed the door shut.

Envying him that he had somewhere safe to retreat to, I seriously doubted he'd open the door for me. The birds would most likely smash through the glass to get to me anyway. I needed somewhere to hide that didn't have windows. The truck was the obvious choice, so I sprinted towards it. Diving inside, I spun around, grabbed the door and slammed it shut. Feeling myself surrounded by boxes, I immediately realized my mistake. The truck was completely lightless and it was crammed so full of produce that I could barely move. I'd just enclosed myself in a metal coffin.

Panic rose at the thought of being trapped. Before I could open the door and jump out, the vehicle was bombarded. The sound of small bodies slamming into the metal walls was deafening. Unable to see anything in the dark interior, I felt the walls closing in around me. I tried to fight my panic, but fear closed its hands around my throat tightly and began to squeeze.

Putting my hands over my ears to block the noise, I didn't realize that I was screaming at first. Even when I heard peal after peal issuing from my mouth, I still couldn't stop. Being imprisoned in a small space was my greatest fear.

The truck rocked from side to side and the contents of the boxes were tossed onto me. I flinched every time something splattered on me and screamed even louder. It felt like the barrage lasted forever before it finally petered out.

It wasn't easy to get my screams under control, but I finally choked them off. Throwing the door open, I tumbled out onto the road in a shower of mashed up fruit and vegetables. Something dripped down the back of my neck, making me shudder. I didn't know what it was and I didn't want to know. I was covered in juice, seeds from the produce and, worst of all, bird droppings.

My hair and clothes hadn't been the only casualties of this attack. Birds littered the ground. Not all of them were dead. Some of them were just stunned from their suicidal dive bombing. Others flapped their wings feebly. Broken and mangled, they would never be able to fly again.

Hearing the mocking caw of the raven, I saw it perched on a street sign and sent it a glare of pure hatred. This was its way of getting even after I'd half-blinded it. I just hoped it never knew how badly its revenge had affected me.

Picking up an apple, I pushed myself to my knees and threw it as hard as I could. The raven gave a startled squawk and ducked just in time. The apple hit the wall behind the bird and splattered into mush. With a final sly glance at me, my feathered nemesis flew away.

Brie appeared beside me and I started back. Seeing the state I was in, she bent over in laughter. Blinded by tears of joy, it took her a few tries before she could grab hold of my arm and teleport us back to Sophia's store. Still laughing, she let me go then staggered back and pointed at me as I shakily climbed to my feet. "I have never in all my years seen anything as pathetic as you look right now," she gasped.

Still in the grip of shock, I couldn't have predicted what I was going to do next. Taking a step towards her, I put my hand on her chest and shoved her as hard as I could. Her laughter was replaced with a startled shriek as she flew across the room. She hit the wall hard enough to leave a small dent in the drywall, then fell to the carpet.

Leo was sitting alone at the table, gaping at her in shock. Brie's expression was murderous as she lurched to her feet. Springing out of his chair, he darted forward and grabbed his twin by the shoulders to stop her before she could stab me. Her blue sword blazed in her hand, ready to slice me apart.

Sophia and Nathan were absent. I was glad neither of them were here to see me in this state. It was bad enough the two young angels had witnessed my condition.

Drawn by the ruckus, Sam came thumping down the stairs and burst into the room. "What happened?" he asked and examined me in confusion. "Are you hurt?"

Apart from a few pecks and scratches, I wasn't physically hurt, but I was about as far from being okay as I'd ever been. Unable to speak without gibbering, I shook my head and walked past him into the kitchen. I took the stairs up to the second floor. The stairwell was dark and narrow and seemed to have doubled in length. I cringed as the walls seemed to close in around me.

Entering the bathroom at the end of the hall, I left the door standing open wide. I stripped off my coat and boots, then climbed into the shower still clothed. I couldn't stand the thought of being enclosed and left the shower curtain open. Turning the water on as hot as I could bear it, I stood beneath the spray with my head bowed and my heart still hammering.

I didn't hear it when Sam and Leo entered the room. I only knew they'd arrived when they climbed into the shower and wrapped their arms around me. Trembling in the aftermath, I was too overwrought to cry. I let them hold me as they offered me their silent comfort.

A few minutes passed before I heard a knock on the door. I didn't bother to raise my head, I knew it had to be Sophia. Brie was probably still downstairs, laughing herself into a coma. Nathan wouldn't have knocked. He would have walked into the room and wrapped me in his arms just like the two boys had done.

"What happened to her?" Sophia asked. Her tone was concerned and maternal.

"We do not know," Leo answered as he gently stroked my hair. Even though he was a male version of Brie, I didn't blame him for his twin's actions. Their faces might look the same, but their personalities couldn't have been more different.

Sam was humming something beneath his breath. His chin was resting on my shoulder and his cheek was pressed up against mine. He wasn't quite as hideous as he had been when he'd first joined us, but he was far from handsome. I'd grown used to the fact that he was an imp and knew that his exterior didn't match his interior. He had a huge heart and he loved me like a sister. Leo loved me, too, in his own way.

"Whatever it was, Brie had something to do with it," Sam said darkly.

I heard Sophia sigh even above the water that cascaded over me. She wasn't surprised that Brie and I had had a falling out. It had been bound to happen sooner or later. "I will take care of her," she offered. "You two can wait for us downstairs."

They were reluctant to leave, but they obeyed her anyway. Sam patted me on the back and kissed me on the cheek before leaving. Leo squeezed my hand in reassurance, then he left as well.

Sophia closed the door and turned the water off so

we could talk. "Violet, can you please open your eyes?" I did as she asked and her face softened when she saw my tightly controlled panic. "Did Briathos do something to you?"

I hesitated, then shook my head. "She wasn't directly responsible." My voice was husky from my panicked screams.

Picking something out of my hair, she examined it before dropping it into the drain at my feet. "Do you think you can undress yourself without my help?"

My shock was finally wearing off. The thought of someone stripping me off like I was a child made me shudder. I was far too independent to allow that to happen. "I can manage."

She politely turned her back while I stripped off my t-shirt, jeans and underwear. I squeezed as much water out of them as I could, then handed them to her. Picking my coat up off the floor, she closed the door and left me in peace. Leo must have used his power to dry both himself and Sam off. Neither of them had left watery footprints on the floor.

I still couldn't bring myself to close the curtain, but I switched the water on again. It took me a while to shower off the bird crap and assorted debris that clung to my hair. When I finally felt clean, my skin was bright pink from the hot water. I shut the shower off and dried myself before anyone could burst inside to check up on me.

Wrapping a towel around my body tightly, I wiped steam off the mirror. Instead of being pink like the rest of my body, my face was far too pale. Fear always seemed to strip me of my color. I hadn't been that terrified for a very long time. I hoped nothing like that would occur again anytime soon. I would rather fight one of the Demon Princes in hell bare-handed than to ever face a situation like that again.

Chapter Three

Dressed only in the damp towel, I combed my hair, but didn't bother to dry it. The wet strands hung almost to my waist. It hadn't been trimmed since I'd fled from Denver. I'd get around to it one day, but I had far more important things to worry about at the moment.

Feeling slightly calmer, I left the bathroom and trudged down the hall to my bedroom. Closing the door and enclosing myself in the room wasn't easy, but I wasn't going to allow myself to be ruled by my terror. I reminded myself that the bathroom was smaller than the bedroom and some of my fear seeped away.

I dressed in a t-shirt, hoodie and jeans, but left my feet bare. The building was heated well enough that socks were optional. I didn't want to head downstairs just yet. I felt embarrassed that my friends had witnessed my meltdown. With my mother dead, no one else knew about my greatest fear. It wasn't something I particularly wanted to talk about.

Searching for a way to delay facing everyone, the flash of red from my ring caught my attention. I stared at the ruby for a few moments. Zach had given it to me as a belated birthday gift. It had been ridiculously expensive, which made me feel even guiltier that I hadn't yet given him anything for his birthday. He'd left town just before Christmas to spend time with family in another state. When we saw each other next, I'd finally be able to give him a gift in return.

Hearing voices raised loudly downstairs, I knew I couldn't put off the inevitable any longer. I hurried into the hall and took the stairs down to the lower level. My bare feet were soundless and the others didn't hear me coming. I paused in the kitchen when Nathan spoke.

"We know you had something to do with whatever happened to Violet," he said in a tone that was bordering on furious. "Tell us what happened to her."

Brie's response was as sulky as any real teenagers would have been. "It was her own fault. She did not listen to me when I was trying to instruct her, so I decided to teach her a lesson."

"What was this lesson that you thought she needed to learn so badly?" my guardian asked. If I were Brie, I would have taken note of his sudden deceptive calm.

"As usual, she was not paying attention to her surroundings. She must learn that she does not possess the same strength and speed that she has in hell when she is here on Earth. She cannot always rely on us to save her when her life is in peril."

"That is what you are here for!" Sam said in my defense. "You are supposed to protect her from danger, not to put her in harm's way!"

"Who are you to lecture me on what I should or should not do, imp?" Her tone had turned as cold as the snow that was settling over the city.

"I am something that you will never be," he said defiantly. "I am her friend. Unlike you, I will always look out for her wellbeing."

"The fact that a lowly creature like you calls himself her friend is exactly the problem," the teen fired back.

"What do you mean?" Leo asked. He sounded like he was striving for patience.

"Violet has no sense of the danger that she puts both herself, and us, in on a daily basis with her sheer ineptitude and the consistently poor choices that she makes." Brie took a breath to calm herself before speaking in a more controlled tone. "Choosing to save that wretched creature from the shadowlands is at the top of the list of stupid things that she has done." I didn't need to see Sam's expression to know he would be hurt by that. Brie wasn't done yet. "She is supposed to be the great and mighty Hellscourge, yet she cannot even tell when a bird is following her."

"Is that what sparked your need to teach her a lesson?" Nathan asked. "The raven was following her and she did not see it?"

I peered through a crack in the door to see Brie nod. "Yes. I spotted it straight away, of course, but she remained clueless. It followed us for several blocks without her knowing about it. I attempted to make her aware of the fact a few times without directly pointing it out to her." I wracked my brain, searching for the clues that she'd apparently given me, and came up blank. Either her clues had been far too subtle for me to pick up on, or she hadn't given me any hints at all.

"So, because she did not see the raven, you decided to allow it to attack her?" Leo asked for clarification.

She nodded and her face cracked into a smile. "You should have seen it. The raven sent a flock of its friends after her. She ran like a child and hid in the back of a truck like a coward. I could hear her screaming in fear while they threw themselves at the vehicle."

I shifted slightly until Nathan came into view. His jaw was clenched and his arms were crossed. "She was not screaming in fear because of the birds," he said tightly.

He knows about my phobia, I realized. It shouldn't have surprised me. He'd been watching over me for a very long time. It made sense that he'd know more about me than I wanted him to. I pushed the door open and stepped inside before he could say anything else. "Don't," I said. "That's my business. She doesn't need to know about it."

Sam rushed over to me and took me by the arm. He helped me over to my seat like I was an invalid. "You look better," he said brightly. It was an attempt to cheer me up that failed miserably.

"I'm fine," I said woodenly. Sophia had made tea and I poured myself a cup. My hands were shaking, but I managed not to spill it.

"Your fear is nothing to be ashamed of," Nathan said gently. "It is only natural after what you went through when you were a child."

I could see Brie out of the corner of my eye, but I refused to look at her directly. She wore a sneer that she probably wasn't even aware of. It was a permanent fixture whenever she looked at me by now. She'd promised to try to be less bitchy, but that hadn't lasted long. "I do not know what happened to cause your fear," she said, "but you are supposed to be the champion of this world. What use will you be if you allow childish terror to rule your emotions?"

It mirrored the thoughts that I'd had when I was getting dressed and I clutched my cup for warmth. She was right, I wasn't a champion. I was just a seventeen-year-old girl who had no business trying to save humanity from the horrible fate that awaited it.

"I would like to know what happened to you to cause your fear," Leo said.

"I think we all would," Sophia agreed.

Sam nodded vigorously. He sat so close beside me

that our arms were touching.

I met Nathan's dark blue eyes and he nodded in support. I blew out a sigh, knowing that I couldn't keep it a secret now. They were my allies as well as my friends, except for Brie. She was just an annoyance that I was forced to deal with on a daily basis. They needed to know my weaknesses as well as my strengths. "I'm pretty sure you were there, so you can tell them the story." I said to Nathan. "I don't really remember all the details anyway." That was a lie. I remembered every moment of the first time that he'd saved my life. It was my earliest memory and it was engraved into my mind forever.

"Violet's mother worked as an aide in a hospital," he began. "She enrolled Violet in daycare so she would have someone to watch over her during the day." His gaze went distant as he recalled the event that had impacted on my life forever. "One of the children was a sadistic little monster. He was only four, yet he was already experimenting with torture."

Sam shifted in his seat and Leo sent me a sympathetic look. They didn't yet know the horror that I'd endured at that little boy's hands, but they were about to find out.

"When I sensed that she was in peril, I went to her immediately. I found her locked in a toy chest that was around this size." He held his hands out to indicate that it had been barely bigger than I'd been at the time. "The little boy was giggling merrily while he held the lid down so she couldn't get out. I cast a spell to make him fall asleep, then rescued Violet. If I had arrived moments later, she would have asphyxiated from a lack of oxygen."

I only vaguely remembered being led over to the chest by the little boy. He'd used the pretense that there was some kind of toy inside. The sensation of his hands on my back as he'd shoved me into the small space came back to haunt me again. He'd shut the lid, plunging me into darkness. I'd instantly panicked and had pounded my tiny hands and feet against the wood in an effort to get out. I could hear the boy, whose name I couldn't remember, laughing in glee. I'd quickly used up my strength, as well as the air.

I'd been on the verge of unconsciousness when the lid had opened and a dim face had appeared above me. I'd been too young to appreciate my guardian angel's beauty at the time, but his face had been mesmerizing. His eyes had been filled with such compassion as he'd picked me up and cradled me against his chest. His wings had wrapped around me for the first time, making me feel safe and cherished.

"How old were you when this happened?" Sam asked. He slid his hand into mine and held on tightly.

I had to clear my throat before I could speak. Memories of the long ago terror had clamped my vocal chords shut. "I was two."

Leo's expression reflected his horror and Sophia's face was wreathed in compassion. "I take it you now suffer from claustrophobia?" she asked.

"Yeah. You could say that."

All eyes shifted to Brie accusingly. "I did not know," she said in self-defense.

Her tone was more defiant than apologetic. It was clear to me that learning why I was claustrophobic hadn't affected her at all. "If you had known, would you have done anything differently?" I asked.

Her hesitation said it all, but she voiced her reasons anyway. "The others coddle you far too much. They treat you as if you are still a child. It is our duty to toughen you up and to ensure that you can face the trials ahead. If this means you will suffer mental as well as physical injuries at times, then so be it."

"You really don't care about me at all, do you?" I said in some wonder. I was amazed that she was so brazenly stating that I meant nothing to her.

Her reply was positively icy. "I do not have the luxury of caring about you. It is your task to stop the gates of hell from being broken open and a flood of demons from being unleashed. The only thing I care about is saving the people of this world from annihilation."

"Well then," I said. "I guess we all know where you stand."

She'd set out to teach me one lesson today and instead I'd learned two. From now on, I would pay more attention and keep a better watch for the raven. The second lesson had been far more important to me. I could no longer depend on Brie to watch my back. I now knew that I would have to keep my eye on her as well. She'd broken my trust with her heartless stunt. I didn't think I would ever be able to forgive her for her cruelty.

Chapter Four

With everyone glaring at her, Brie decided it would be best to vacate the premises until we'd all calmed down. She disappeared to an undisclosed location, which raised a question that had been on my mind. "The wards that keep us all trapped here must be fairly sophisticated," I said.

"What do you mean?" Sam asked.

"Angels and demons can't teleport themselves out of Manhattan, but they can still zap themselves anywhere within the city."

Nathan nodded in agreement. "The hellscribes have developed runes that are more powerful than we had realized."

I had one of the scribes of the underworld squatting inside me. If I'd been in the shadowlands or in hell, I could have spoken to him directly. Since I was currently on Earth, I didn't have that option. "It makes me wonder what other tricks they have up their sleeves."

Leo made a suggestion. "The next time you dream about the legion, perhaps you could ask your scribe exactly what his runes can do."

They'd all taken to calling the demons that were trapped inside me by that nickname. It had started out as a joke, but with each new soul that I ingested, the larger the group became. I had nearly two hundred hell spawn inside me now, and one lone human. I visited Heather from time to time so she would have some company that didn't remind her of the torment that she'd suffered through.

His suggestion was a good one, but I'd already tried it. "I have asked him," I said with a shrug. "He's reluctant to divulge his secrets and I don't want to force him to tell me."

Sophia inclined her head in agreement. "You need him on your side in the event that his abilities become necessary again. You do not want him to turn against you and refuse to offer you his knowledge."

The only reason the legion was willing to assist me at all was because they wanted to survive long enough to be able to escape from me. We were all hoping that I would find a way to release their souls from captivity. If I died, they'd most likely go down with me like rats that didn't have the option of abandoning a sinking ship.

Nathan reached out to touch one of the scratches

that marred my face. As always, he was so gentle that he made my heart ache. "Did you receive any serious injuries during the bird attack?"

I could read the longing in his eyes and felt the same way. He was secretly hoping that he'd have a chance to heal me again. I shook my head. "Nope. I only have a few shallow scratches."

He had the ability to heal me with his kiss, but it was dangerous for him to use his grace that way. Each time he infused me with his power, we both became a little more addicted to the sensation. Ever since I'd learned about the dangers of being healed by him, I'd done my best to avoid being hurt. I'd even gone as far as hiding some of my wounds that I'd received during our skirmishes with demons from him. As a consequence, I had a few more scars now. I'd never planned on a career as a bikini model, so it didn't really matter that my skin wasn't flawless.

Sam pointedly cleared his throat when we'd been staring at each other for a bit too long. Nathan dropped his eyes, breaking me from his spell. With his chin length black hair, sharp cheekbones and sensual lips, he was stunning. I wasn't alone in being drawn to him. Other women were just as susceptible to his good looks. I'd caught more than a few of them staring at him whenever we went out on patrol together. Some had to be at least twice his vessel's age, which was around nineteen.

"I should go and check on Briathos," he said and was gone before we could say anything. He could find her as long as she was wearing her bracelet. He had a talent for tracking spells that other angels didn't seem to possess.

Leo and Sophia exchanged a glance, then they both turned to me. I held up my hand before they could verbalize their warnings. "I know. Nathan is off limits. You don't have to remind me about it." One thing I couldn't stand was being lectured to as if I was an ignorant child. It was one of the reasons I'd never gotten along with any of my teachers.

Sophia poured herself some tea and I offered my cup for a refill. She chose her words carefully before speaking. "I am afraid it will not be easy for you two to resist your feelings for each other," she said as delicately as possible.

"We've managed to resist them so far," I said with a frown.

"Sophia and I think you were right about something that you said recently," Leo said.

"You mean you guys actually listen to me?" I said in a mutter that they heard just fine.

"We always listen to you," Sophia replied primly.

"What did I say that you think I'm right about?"

Leo leaned forward and rested his elbows on the table. "You said that the longer we stay inside our vessels, the more attuned we become to them. Brie and I have a habit of being childish from time to time, exactly as if we were real teenagers."

I remembered saying something along those lines. "What does that have to do with Nathan and me?"

"Nathanael is possessing the body of a young man," the clairvoyant said. "His vessel has all of the usual needs and desires of any human male."

My mouth dropped open at her implication. "He wouldn't let his vessel take control and do anything stupid." Kissing me to heal me was one thing. What she was talking about went way beyond just making out.

Leo smiled, but it wasn't joyful. "If he were a normal angel, you would be right about that. Unfortunately, I fear he is not the same as we are anymore."

Sophia's expression turned wistful as he included her. She'd lost her grace and wasn't technically an angel at all anymore.

"What aren't you telling me?" I asked suspiciously. I knew Nathan was from a different order of the angelic hierarchy than Brie and Leo, but I hadn't learned anything more than that so far. I wasn't quite brave enough to ask him outright.

"That is Nathan's tale to tell you," Sophia said firmly. "We just feel that you should try not to allow yourself to become too close to him."

That ship had already sailed, but I nodded to appease them. I'd read a book about what happened when male angels used their vessels to mate with human women. The females had fallen pregnant and had given birth to a race of giants called the Nephilim. After reading the horrors that the unnatural offspring had unleashed on the world, I wasn't going to make the same mistake that those poor women had. I was pretty sure I was in love with my guardian, but I wouldn't allow myself to act on my feelings. For both of our sakes, it was best for us to keep our distance as much as possible.

Sam had his mind on other matters and voiced them. "I cannot believe what Brie did to you." His expression was as dark as his tone.

"She didn't exactly make the raven and its feathered friends attack me," I said grudgingly. Defending her was the last thing I wanted to do, but she wasn't really to blame here. Sure, her actions were questionable, but the undead bird was at fault.

Sitting stiffly in the seat next to me, he stubbornly refused to cut her any slack. "She could have found another way to teach you the lesson that she believed you needed to learn so badly. She did not have to allow you to suffer such torment."

Leo came to his twin's defense. "Brie did not know about Violet's claustrophobia." He sent me a hurt look that I'd kept them in the dark. "None of us did."

Holding my cup, I shrugged carefully so I didn't spill my tea. "It isn't exactly something I wanted everyone to know about."

"You do not trust us?" Sam asked hesitantly.

"Of course I trust you." The only one I didn't trust now was Brie. I bumped my shoulder against his affectionately. "I guess I just don't want you to know that I'm weak."

Leo frowned at that. "Having a phobia does not

mean you are weak. It simply means that you are human."

"I suppose angels don't have any fears," I said with a sigh.

"We have fears," he refuted. "Brie named one of them before she disappeared to sulk in private."

"You're afraid I'm going to lose this war and that mankind will be doomed," I said softly.

He fell silent, but I read the confirmation in his bleak expression.

Chapter Five

Sam headed upstairs to watch one of his beloved TV shows and I tagged along behind him. His addiction to television had increased. He was glued to the couch night and day, unless he was training.

At my insistence, he managed to tear himself away to practice combat for a couple of hours a day. His skills had improved, but he was far from being a warrior. Whatever fighting ability he'd had as a pirate had been forgotten long ago. He'd learned a different set of skills during his imprisonment in hell. His ability to become almost invisible had saved us both many times. Brie was wrong to say it had been a mistake to drag him out of the shadowlands. Rescuing Sam was the best decision I'd ever made.

He plonked down on the comfortable brown sofa and I stepped across the hall into my bedroom.

Checking that no one was watching me, I dug my cell phone out of my pocket and checked for messages. I felt a small glow of happiness when I saw a text from Zach. He was back in town and he wanted to see me tomorrow at one in the afternoon.

It was Sam's turn to escort me on patrol tomorrow, which would make it easier for me to meet my boyfriend. I texted back that I could make it and asked him where he wanted to meet me. His response was a surprise. He told me to meet him around the corner from his apartment building. I sent an agreement to the plan, wondering why he hadn't arranged to meet at our usual spot. We tended to use a café that was popular enough for us to become lost in the crowd.

Meeting with Zach was always a risk now. My relationship with him wasn't quite as secret as I would have liked. After one of my dates with him, I'd been kidnapped by a couple of angels by the name of Hagith and Orifiel. I'd nicknamed them Hag and Orifice just to piss them off. They'd warned me to keep my mind on the job and had threatened to do something to either me, or to Zach if I allowed myself to become too distracted by him. For all I knew, they were hiding somewhere nearby so they could follow me every time I left Sophia's store.

Even with their threat hanging over me, I couldn't bring myself to end things with Zach. He was the only thing that I had left from my old life. I'd lost everything when the demons had killed my mother and I'd been forced to flee from Denver. I wasn't going to let them take him away from me as well. The few times I managed to sneak away to see him were the only instances when I had any normalcy these days.

Sam glanced at me when I entered the living room. "You look happy," he said slyly as I took a seat on the armchair.

I pretended to be nonchalant. "Do I?"

"Does this mean your beau has finally returned?"

I made a face at his archaic wording, but I knew he was only teasing me. Nathan had used the same term to refer to Zach when he'd first joined our team. I was doing my best to bring both the imp and the angels into the twenty-first century. Sadly, they all still spoke as if they were living in another era. "Zach is back in town," I confirmed quietly.

"When have you arranged to meet with him?"

"Tomorrow at one."

"That is fortunate," he mused. "This means we will not have to resort to subterfuge this time."

"Are you sure you'll be able to tear yourself away from the TV for a few hours?" I teased him.

His expression became conflicted as he realized he'd be gone from the store for so long. "Your safety is more important than watching my favorite shows," he said and sounded as if he was trying to convince himself of that.

Fortunately, my boyfriend was on board with the idea of keeping our relationship a secret. I was still a wanted felon. His father had posted a bodyguard to watch Zach just in case I tried to make contact with him. Giles, his creepy chauffeur slash stalker, followed him everywhere. Zach had to sneak away every time we met, which restricted how often we could see each other.

When I fell asleep later that night, I tried to visit the shadowlands that I'd created for the legion. They remained stubbornly absent. I had little control over my dreams, but I usually ended up there sooner or later. It happened more frequently when I was in some kind of trouble. With things being eerily quiet the way they were at the moment, my brain tended to rest while I was asleep.

It was hard to act normal during breakfast the next morning. I gave Brie a nasty glare when I took a seat at the table. More because it was expected than out of any real anger. I was too excited at the prospect of seeing Zach to dwell on how much she disliked me. Frankly, the feeling was mutual by now. She felt superior to humans and had never pretended to think of me as anything less than a mere tool. Now that she'd all-but admitted that out loud, there was no more need for me to act friendly towards her.

After breakfast, I spent two hours training with Leo. It was hard to stay focused, but it helped to pass the time. When we were done, he called Sam down for his turn. We used sticks that had once been a broom handle to attack each other with. Injuries weren't completely eliminated, but they were greatly reduced.

Poor Sam was almost as inept as I had been when I'd first started learning how to defend myself. Without the demonic dwellers inside me, I was fairly sure I'd still be just as hopeless as I'd first been. It took years of training to gain the skill to battle demons. Thanks to my strange quirk of being able to absorb souls, I could call on their strength and experience whenever I was in need. As Brie had pointed out, their abilities were muted while I was on Earth. It was a different story when I was in the shadowlands and in hell. They could take control of my limbs and use them directly once we were in their dimension, as long as I gave them permission to.

Brie stood to one side with her arms crossed, glaring at the wall. Clearly, she was in a bad mood. Nathan sat at the table, watching the action without really seeing it. Every now and then, his gaze would slide across to me. I resisted the temptation to look straight at him. Sophia watched us both with a small frown that she probably wasn't even aware of. She knew we had feelings for each other and was understandably concerned that we'd make a horrible mistake and take things too far.

When Leo finally called a halt to their training session, I waited for Sam to glance at me and surreptitiously nodded towards the door. He nodded back and headed upstairs to change. When he returned, he was wearing a long black coat that was nearly identical to mine. Sophia supplied us with our clothing, so I couldn't really complain that we looked so similar. Speaking of my coat, it was hanging on the front door. Either Leo or Nathan must have cleaned off the crap that it had been covered with. Not even a washing machine would have been able to get rid of all of the gunk that had been splattered on me when I'd been attacked by the birds.

"Do we have to go out today?" I whined. I hoped I wasn't overacting my reluctance.

"Yes," Sam said firmly. "You need your exercise and you also need to practice making sure you are not being followed. After all, you would not want to have to be taught another lesson." He sent a poisonous glare at Brie.

Her back immediately stiffened, but Sophia sent her a warning look before she could explode into an angry tirade. The teen hated the imp even more than she despised me, if that was even possible.

"Make sure you keep her safe," Nathan instructed him.

We all heard the unspoken threat behind his words. I wasn't sure what he would do to Sam if I came to any harm. I would have to do my best to make sure that I returned in one piece. "We'll be fine," I said and headed for the door. "We're going to check out the Upper East Side. We haven't been there for a while."

Leo looked disturbed with good reason. "Stay away from Central Park. That is where the raven seems to have made its nest."

I nodded, then stepped outside. Sam was right behind me. I'd told them the truth about where we were heading just in case they decided to check up on us. After seeing what happened to souls who lied, I preferred to stick to the truth as much as possible these days.

Brie's lesson yesterday had been harsh, but it had had the effect that she'd wanted. I scanned the sky, buildings, street signs, lamp posts and anywhere else a bird could use as a perch. So far, the raven hadn't managed to follow us back to our lair, but that might not even be necessary for it to find out where our base was. It had scratched me with its talons a few weeks ago, which had forged a connection between us. Its master had been able to infiltrate Sophia's store just enough to give me a fright.

Seeing the face of the current leader of hell on a tarot-like card had been a shock that I wouldn't soon forget. Brie had cleansed the store to banish the evil and it hadn't returned so far. Sophia hadn't told her the exact reason why she'd wanted the spell to be cast. She'd just given her the excuse that it might strengthen the wards that only angels could see.

Sam searched the sky as diligently as I did. We both pulled our hoods up to keep the light snow out of our faces. We did our best not to be too obvious about searching for anyone or anything that might be watching us.

Our clothing was generic enough to help us blend in with the few pedestrians that were on the sidewalks. I kept my long blond hair tucked beneath my hood. It stood out too much to allow anyone to see it. The stone bracelets we both wore would keep us hidden from demons, but it didn't work against angels. Hag and Orifice could be following us right now and we would never even know it.

"Do you feel like someone is watching us?" I asked my companion.

Sam's face was hidden deep inside his hood. He glanced around again. "No. Do you?"

"I'm not sure. Maybe I'm just being paranoid."

"You have a good reason to be. You have many enemies and they all want you dead."

"They don't *all* want me dead," I reminded him as we made our way towards Fifth Ave. "The Hellmaster seems to want me alive."

His coat rustled when he shuddered in fear. "I do not understand why he has instructed his minions to bring you to him unharmed."

That made two of us. It was a pity the Hellmaster's lackeys no longer seemed to want to follow his orders when it came to me. I'd been named Hellscourge for a very good reason. When I was in their domain, I could end their existence. Now that they were aware that they were no longer immortal, they were terrified. I'd killed the prince of the eighth realm and desperation had spread throughout demonkind. Most of them were determined to kill me before I could kill them.

Chapter Six

Fifth Avenue was great for window shopping, but it tended to wreak havoc on the bank account. I'd only ever been inside one of the stores along this prestigious street. My attention had been drawn to the only ring that had a sparkling ruby in it. Zach had caught me staring at it and had insisted on buying it for me.

I touched my coat pocket where I'd slipped the present that I'd bought for him. I felt nervous at the thought of handing it over. My mother was the only person I'd ever bought gifts for in the past. I was horribly lonely without her, but at least I had some friends now. They helped fill the void that had been left inside me with her death.

Having friends was still a relatively new experience for me. Zach had been the only one who had befriended me at my school in Denver. I'd always been a loner who'd been ostracized by the other kids. I knew why now. My soul had been stripped away, leaving an empty shell behind. Humans sensed that something was wrong with me and tended to avoid me like the plague.

At least, I assumed my soul had been stolen. Perhaps I'd been born without one. Maybe that was why I'd been chosen to be Hellscourge. Fate had told me that I was different from everyone else, but she hadn't specified how or why. As far as I knew, every other being on the planet had a soul.

Taking Leo's advice to avoid Central Park, we swung eastward just before we reached the stone fence that ran around the perimeter of the grounds. We cut across to Maddison Ave and headed north again. Zach's apartment building was on the corner of Park Ave and one of the side streets.

Sam melted out of sight when we reached the side street. He used his camouflage abilities to become nearly invisible against a brick wall. He would keep watch from a distance to give me the privacy that I needed.

Zach was waiting for me around the corner from the main entrance to his building. His blond hair made a stark contrast to his black clothing. He wore a coat that was a lot more expensive than mine. All of his clothing was tailor made. I was pretty sure his shoes were also custom made. He could afford the best of everything, while I wore cheap clothing that had been bought during clearance sales.

I waved to get his attention. His face lit up in a smile and he gestured for me to follow him. To my surprise, he didn't lead the way to a nearby coffee shop. Instead, he opened a side door to his building and stepped inside. He tore something off the latch while I scanned the street for the raven or for Giles the bodyguard. Neither of them were lurking around. "What was that?" I asked, gesturing at the object that he'd slipped into his pocket.

"I put tape on the latch to make sure the door didn't lock behind me," he said and grinned at his cleverness.

"Were you a burglar in a former life?" I joked.

He shook his head. "Nah. I saw it on TV."

I glanced back up the street to see Sam materialize for a moment. He was worried about me entering the building alone, but I sent him a reassuring smile. I'd been dying of curiosity about this place ever since I'd discovered that Zach lived here. It was one of the most expensive apartment buildings in the city. I'd walked past the foyer a few times and had been astounded by the sheer opulence. The chance to actually take a look inside was too tempting for me to resist.

Following Zach inside, I was disappointed to find myself in a plain corridor that could have belonged inside any building. The walls were dark gray and the floor was covered in plain black tiles. There were no decorations at all.

Zach put a finger to his lips, cautioning me to be quiet as he took the lead. We turned a corner into another hallway and ended up at a flight of stairs leading up. We climbed up to the second floor before emerging into a very different hallway. Deep maroon carpet covered the floor. The walls were a matching shade of maroon and several paintings were on display.

"Wait here for a second," he murmured and crossed to the elevator to push the button. It arrived moments later and opened to reveal an empty interior. "Hurry," he said and I darted across to join him. "Stand on the other side of the elevator and pretend you don't know me," he whispered as I entered the confines of the metal box. He pushed the button for the eighteenth and twentieth floors.

Following his directions, I stood across from him. We both took our cell phones out and did our best to act casually. The maroon carpet extended inside the elevator. It was thick enough to make anyone wearing high heels unsteady on their feet. My boots were only an inch high. Fighting in heels was beyond my abilities. Trying to run in them would probably result in a broken ankle. Speed and safety were more important to me than being trendy.

A camera looked down at us from one corner. I snuck peeks at the mirrored walls and saw myself reflected from every angle. Zach caught my eye and fought to smother a grin. I hid my smile as best as I could and pretended to be engrossed in my cell phone again.

The ride was too short for me to become paralyzed with a panic attack from claustrophobia. Still, sweat broke out onto my brow when the walls seemed to be closing in on me. I glanced up and was grateful to see we were approaching the eighteenth floor.

Zach raised his hand to his mouth to cover a fake yawn. "The stairs are to the left and around the corner," he whispered. "I'll meet you on the twentieth floor."

I stepped out and the door whisked shut, leaving me on my own. Growing more nervous by the second, I hurried down the hallway to where the stairs were tucked around the corner. There didn't seem to be any security cameras in the hallways. The stairs were unlocked, just as Zach had promised. I climbed up to the top as I'd been instructed.

He was waiting for me when I pushed the door open. His smile was mischievous as he led me around the corner. A door stood directly across from the elevator. It was the only one in sight. It was massive and was made of black wood. It reminded me of the petrified wood that was used in hell and I suppressed a shudder. I'd seen two female demons enter this building once. Both had been captains of hell's armies. They could be hiding anywhere inside the structure.

Unlocking the door, he pushed it open wide. "Welcome to my home," he said. He grinned when my mouth dropped open. The dimple in his left cheek appeared, making him almost unbearably adorable.

I gaped in stunned amazement as I took in the gigantic open space. The floor was black marble that was shot through with gold. The walls were a gray that was so dark it was almost as black as the floor. It was a little too dark and masculine for my tastes. Without the subtle lighting that shone down from the high ceiling, the apartment would have been almost gloomy.

Dark, antique furniture stood in strategic places near the walls. Expensive, but comfortable looking black leather couches surrounded a massive TV to the left. A formal dining room was straight ahead with a table that could seat twenty. It was also black and had a glossy, reflective finish. An actual grand piano stood in a corner. It was as black as the floor and I didn't see it at first. The ivory keys caught my eye. They seemed to float in midair at first glance.

The paintings in here made the ones in the hallways downstairs look like cheap replicas. Marble statues of men and women wearing robes and little else sat on pedestals. The pure white stone made a startling contrast to all the black. They had to be worth a fortune. More subtle lighting highlighted the artwork, drawing my eyes to them one by one and capturing my attention completely.

"What do you think?" Zach asked anxiously when I remained mute.

"I've never seen anything like this before," I replied honestly. "I didn't even know people lived in this sort of luxury."

He shrugged in embarrassment and drew me inside before closing the door. "If you think this is luxurious, wait until you see the bathrooms." He said it with a smile, but I was pretty sure he wasn't joking.

I desperately wanted to have a tour of his home, but I was cautious. "Isn't it dangerous for me to be here? What if someone sees me?" An apartment this big would surely have staff employed to look after it.

"My father will be away for a few hours and our housekeeper is out running errands. She won't be back until later this afternoon."

This seemed too good to be true. My luck wasn't usually this good. "What if they come back early and catch me here?"

Holding up his cell phone, his expression held a hint of smugness. "I've tapped into our security system. My phone will alert us if anyone enters the apartment. I'll distract whoever enters, giving you a clear path so you can sneak out without being spotted."

"What are you? Some kind of hacker?" I was only half joking. I hadn't known he had tech skills like this.

"I wish," he replied ruefully. "You can find out how to do almost anything if you search the internet." His hair was sexily disheveled from waiting for me out in the wind. His eyes were brown, which was an unusual combination with his blond hair. He was nearly six feet tall and his shoulders seemed to be getting wider by the day.

Realizing we'd been staring at each other for a while, he blushed. "I'm being a terrible host. Let me take your coat, then I'll give you a tour."

Slipping out of my coat, I half turned away and transferred his gift to the back pocket of my jeans. He'd shrugged out of his coat as well and draped both garments over his arm. My boots were slightly dirty and I wasn't about to walk across the immaculate floors. I toed them off and picked them up. Zach's shoes were clean. The sidewalk outside his apartment building was swept frequently to keep it clear of snow.

We walked through the foyer and headed to the right. He showed me an enormous kitchen with gleaming stainless steel appliances. An island counter took up nearly a third of the room. It was large enough to host a dinner party on.

We made our way through each room, pausing so I could examine everything. He showed me another dining room that was less formal and a second living room with a slightly smaller TV. Just as he'd promised, the bathrooms were breathtaking. Black and gold marble was the predominant décor in all four bathrooms. The tubs came equipped with jets that could massage the occupant from all sides. They were large enough for several people to fit inside and the showers were the same. Everything was modern, yet somehow classical. I felt too poor and shabby to even step inside his home, let alone to touch anything.

Finished touring the main section, we ended up in

the formal dining room again. Seeing a wide doorway beyond the glossy black table, I peered through the windows to see a balcony outside. The balcony was large enough to host a family barbeque. The balustrade was made of intricate stonework. I realized that this was the balcony that had so impressed me when I'd first discovered that Zach was in the city. I was standing in the very penthouse that I'd longed to see.

Zach pointed to a doorway across the room to the left of the main area that we hadn't been inside yet. "My Dad's rooms are through there." I'd never met his father and hadn't even seen a photo of him yet. There were no family photos anywhere. Instant curiosity rose, but it would be idiotic to sneak into his dad's room. Doing so would almost guarantee that he'd come home early and bust us in the act of snooping. The cops in Denver had undoubtedly shown him my photo. His father would be able to turn me in if he ever saw me.

"My rooms are this way," he said and took my hand. With an inviting smile, he led me through the door on the far side of the apartment.

Chapter Seven

I shouldn't have been surprised that Zach had an entire wing to himself, but I hadn't realized just how big the penthouse was. We stepped through the door into a short hallway. Turning a corner to the right, we passed a few doorways until we reached a bedroom at the far end of the hall.

He pushed the door open and moved aside to let me in first. Again, I could only stare in wonder at first. Instead of maroon, dark blue carpet covered the floor. It was almost the exact same shade of blue as Nathan's eyes. I shoved that thought aside. I was determined to keep my guardian out of my thoughts while I was with my boyfriend. It wasn't fair to Zach for me to be thinking about another man while I was spending time with him.

A TV was mounted on the wall to our left. It was

just as large as the one in the main living area. A long sofa in dark brown leather and a black coffee table with a glass top were the only living room furniture. A few paintings hung on the walls, which were painted in a shade of blue that was a few tones lighter than the carpet.

I saw four doors that I hadn't explored yet, but it was the bed that drew my attention. King-size, it was black and modern and was covered in a royal blue comforter. Several pillows were haphazardly stacked against the bedhead. It sat directly across from the door and had black bedside tables on either side. "Your bed is big enough for four people," I marveled.

His eyes went dreamy. "I'd be happy to settle for just the two of us."

Flustered, I broke eye contact with him. We'd resumed dating after I'd run into him a few weeks ago, but I'd asked him to take things slowly. The demons that were locked in my head were changing me in ways that I hadn't anticipated. They'd awakened my lust and it was triggered every time Zach kissed me. It was different with Nathan. I found his touch to be blissful rather than filling me with the need to devour him. Both feelings were strong and they were almost impossible to control.

Zach hung my coat up in a closet next to the entrance. I placed my boots on a mat that had been specifically designed to hold wet or muddy shoes. He took his shoes off and placed them next to mine, then drew me over to a set of curtains to the left of the bed. I gasped when he drew them aside to reveal his own private balcony behind a set of French doors.

"Can we go outside?" I asked. Snow was still falling, but only lightly.

"It'll be freezing out there," he warned me, but he pulled the doors open anyway. I stepped out onto the gray stones. Even with socks on, my feet turned numb almost instantly on the freezing surface. He followed me and shut the door to keep the snow out of his room. Crossing to the railing, it was cold beneath my bare hands. I leaned over and looked down to see the ground dizzyingly far below. Unlike the Empire State Building, fences hadn't been erected to prevent suicide. It would be far too easy to fall from this balcony.

Zach slid his hands around my waist and held onto me tightly as if he was afraid I was going to jump. I sent him a reassuring smile. No matter how bad things had gotten, or how deep my depression had become after I'd seen my mother murdered, the thought of committing suicide had never crossed my mind.

"The view is amazing," I said as I scanned the neighborhood. I could see Central Park two streets away to the west. It was covered in several inches of snow and had become a winter wonderland.

My smile withered and died when I caught sight of something moving out of the corner of my eye. I knew what I would see even before I turned. I watched in trepidation as the raven landed on the building right across the street from me. It was perched on the railing of the balcony with its single milky eye fixed on my face. I didn't know how it kept finding me, but it seemed to turn up whenever I stopped in one spot for a while.

"You're cold," Zach said when I shivered. He hadn't noticed the demonic bird yet and I didn't want him to see it. "We should go back inside before you get pneumonia."

I didn't argue with him. The view was no longer magical now that I knew my nemesis was lurking right outside. We went back in and I pulled the curtains shut so it wouldn't be able to spy on us. It was bad enough that it knew where I was. I didn't want it to watch my every move as well. I just hoped it wouldn't call on backup to ambush me when I left the building.

"Do you want some tea?" he asked.

"Are you going to call a servant from somewhere in the building to deliver it?" I teased. I was determined not to let the arrival of the Hellmaster's spy ruin our date.

"I'm not quite that helpless." He pointed at a door to the right of the entrance. "I have my own kitchen, so we don't even have to leave my rooms."

I rolled my eyes at that. "Of course you have your own kitchen. You probably have your own personal chef, too."

He looked away guiltily, which confirmed my guess. "You must think I'm the most spoiled person you've ever met."

"Pretty much," I replied honestly and slid my arm through his. "But I'll try not to hold it against you. It's not your fault your Dad is filthy rich."

His smile was uncertain at first, but he gained confidence when he saw that I meant it. Most girls would have been ecstatic to date someone with his apparently obscene level of wealth. I found it more annoying than enticing. If he'd been just a normal guy, we wouldn't have had to sneak around like this. His father wouldn't have been able to afford a bodyguard to stalk his son and make sure he didn't run into any unsavory characters like me.

When we stepped into his kitchen, I couldn't deny that his father's money had perks. He had a fancy looking coffee machine that could make several different types of the horrible brew. "That thing almost makes me wish I liked coffee," I said in admiration. The electric kettle that stood beside it looked pathetic in comparison.

"I can't believe you don't drink coffee," he replied as he switched the kettle on. "Are you sure you're human?"

His question unknowingly hit a chord and I had to muster up a smile. Sometimes, I wasn't sure what I was. "Maybe I just have a more refined palate than you do," I said archly.

He stared at me incredulously. "Your favorite meal is a hamburger and fries."

I sniggered and didn't bother to deny it. "I suppose you have lobster and caviar every night." I hadn't had the pleasure of eating either substance, but I wasn't sure I really wanted to. I could eat fish, but other types of seafood didn't really appeal to me.

"Not every night," he countered. "We only eat it on special occasions." Switching topics, he gestured at the full-sized refrigerator. "Are you hungry?"

"Always." I wasn't ashamed to admit that I could eat. I'd always had a fast metabolism and tended to burn food off quickly.

"Grab whatever you want," he offered, then went about making us both tea. He'd taken to drinking tea when he was with me after learning just how much I detested the taste of coffee. It did things to a person's breath that I didn't find particularly attractive.

Finding cheese on a shelf in the fridge, I searched the cupboard until I located crackers. It wasn't a fancy meal, but I arranged them on a plate and followed Zach over to the couch. He put our mugs on the coffee table, then fished his cell phone out of his pocket. He placed it within reach on the table. Now we wouldn't have to worry about missing the alert if anyone entered the apartment.

"What did you do for Christmas?" he asked when we'd made ourselves comfortable.

We sat facing each other with our legs entwined. I'd propped cushions behind me and he'd done the same. I made a face at his question. "Sophia doesn't celebrate the holiday."

He was astonished to hear that. "So, you didn't do anything at all?"

"Nope." I shrugged to indicate that it didn't bother me, but it did a little. Even though I'd been surrounded by my friends, I'd still felt lonely during the holiday. "What about you? Did you enjoy yourself?"

"I spent most of my time with my cousins." He didn't look happy about it. "They're even more spoiled than I am, the obnoxious little monsters."

"Sounds awesome," I said wistfully and reached for a cracker and some cheese. He copied me and we ate in silence for a while. Neither of us had any siblings, but at least he had cousins that were around his age to annoy him. With my mother dead, I had no relatives left that I knew of. Zach's parents had divorced when he'd been small and his father had won custody of him. His mother had moved somewhere overseas and he hadn't seen her in years. I had the feeling his father had high expectations and wanted him to follow in his footsteps. "Did you get many gifts?" I asked at last.

"Loads of them," he replied with a laugh. His mirth faded and he looked at me intently. "Speaking of gifts, I have something for you."

I groaned to hear that. "You've already spent way too much on me!" I pointed at the ring that had probably cost him a small fortune.

"Does it look like money is a problem for me?" he asked philosophically and waved a hand at the opulence that surrounded us.

"No. But I don't want you to feel like you have to

buy me things."

"It's too late for that," he replied with a cheeky grin and reached into the back pocket of his trousers. "I love giving you gifts. Besides, what sort of boyfriend would I be if I didn't get you a Christmas present?"

I took the small box reluctantly. It had been expertly wrapped by a professional and I was almost afraid to open it. Tearing the wrapping off, I opened the box and blinked when I saw the contents. Instead of the expensive piece of jewelry that I'd expected, a leather bracelet was nestled inside. Three strips of leather had been inexpertly plaited and the ends had been crudely tied together. It had clearly been homemade by someone with little experience with leatherwork.

Zach's expression grew anxious when I picked it up. "I made it myself," he said bashfully. "You don't have to wear it if you don't want to."

It was far from pretty, but my eyes blurred with tears anyway. I slipped it over my left wrist to sit snugly beside my watch. The fact that he'd gone to the trouble to make something for me touched me deeply. "I love it," I said and leaned forward to kiss him. I kept the contact brief so I couldn't become overwhelmed with lust. "I have something for you, too."

He looked surprised, but pleased. "You didn't have to get me anything."

"What kind of girlfriend would I be if I didn't get you a combined birthday and Christmas present?" I said teasingly. I reached inside my pocket for a box that was similar to the one he'd given me. The wrapping that I'd used was cheap, just like the present that lay inside it. I was hoping that the thought would mean as much to him as his leather bracelet meant to me.

Zach took it from me and tore the wrapping off. He opened the box and stared down at the necklace that I'd bought him only a few days ago. I'd seen it while I'd been out on patrol with Sam. It was a fire opal on a leather chain that looked a lot like the bracelet that he'd made for me, but far better formed.

"Turn it over," I urged.

He did and ran a finger over the engraving that was on the back. The metal was only silver, but it was the closest thing to a ruby set in platinum that I could afford. "What do these symbols mean?" he asked.

They were my initials in the equivalent of the demons' alphabet. Entwined together, they looked a lot like a demon rune, but I couldn't tell him that. "They don't mean anything," I shrugged. "I saw them in a dream." That much was true. I'd had a conversation with my hellscribe and he'd described them to me. Looking around the room at the expensive things that surrounded us, I wouldn't have blamed Zach for throwing the paltry gift back in my face. "I know it isn't much," I said, suddenly doubtful.

"Material things don't mean a lot to me," he said. "I've been showered with meaningless gifts my entire life. This is the first thing that anyone has given me that came from the heart." He hesitated for a moment, turning bashful. "It did come from your heart, didn't it?"

I melted at the vulnerability I saw in his dark eyes. "Of course it did."

He grinned in relief at my admission. "Then this is the best gift that I've ever received." He pulled me in for a kiss and my lust was instantly ignited. A small voice told me to be careful, but it was drowned out by the heat that was rapidly rising inside me.

Chapter Eight

My hands slid into Zach's hair and I deepened the kiss. Our tea was forgotten and so was my common sense. I crawled onto his lap and wrapped myself around him. His hands roamed up and down my back as our tongues became reacquainted. We were both breathing heavily and our pulses were racing.

I wasn't sure how much time had passed when a beeping sound finally intruded on our make-out session. Zach's hands were beneath my shirt. He'd just unhooked my bra and his hands were sliding around my sides. In another second or two, he would have held my breasts in his palms.

Cold reason hit me and I jerked away at the thought of him discovering the ugly scar on my left breast. "What's that noise?" I said, trying to hide my fear of him finding out about what I thought of as a deformity.

"Huh?" His expression was dazed and his eyes were glazed with passion. Then he heard the noise and his face went pale. He reached out to pick up his phone and looked at the screen. "My Dad's home and he's heading this way," he said in a horrified whisper. The color fled from my face as well at that news. "Hide!" he said and I scrambled to my feet.

Turning in a circle, I spied the closet door standing open. Snatching up my boots from the mat, I darted inside just as a knock came at the door. Putting my boots down, I hiked my shirt up and reached behind me to do my bra up. I watched through a crack as Zach slid his new necklace into his pocket. He jabbed a button on his phone to shut the alarm off and smoothed his hair down. Seeing my cup sitting next to his on the coffee table, he hastily placed it behind the couch where it wouldn't be seen. His body had reacted to rubbing up against mine and that wasn't something he could easily hide. He crossed his legs and assumed an innocent expression. "Come in!" he said loudly.

The door opened inwards, blocking his father from my view when he poked his head inside. "My meeting ended early," he said in a deep baritone. "I thought you might like to go out for dinner tonight. Clarice Weller and her daughter, Candice, will be joining us." He said this as if it was incentive for his son to accompany him.

"Sure," Zach said with a pleasant smile. "What time

will we be leaving?"

"Eight. I have business to attend to first. Make sure you wear a suit." With that order, he closed the door.

I waited until his footsteps had faded before leaving the closet. "Who are Clarice and Candice Weller?" I asked.

Zach flushed and ran a hand through his hair. "Clarice is one of my father's clients. I think they're trying to fix me up with her daughter, Candice."

"Is she pretty?" I kept my tone neutral, but jealousy was wrapping its ugly claws around me.

"Yeah. She's beautiful and she knows it," he said morosely. "She's exactly the type of girl I try to avoid at all costs; shallow, spoiled and fake."

His answer reassured me and I smiled in relief. "So, I guess you won't be cheating on me with her then?"

He was shocked by that. "I would never cheat on you." He came to his feet and walked over to take my hand. "You're the only one for me, Violet," he said earnestly. "No other girl has ever made me feel the way you do."

We became lost in each other's eyes until I realized that too much time had passed. Someone would come looking for me if I didn't head back to Sophia's store soon. "I have to go," I said reluctantly.

"Wait here, I'll make sure the way is clear." He left his room to check on his father and returned a couple of minutes later. "He's busy in his office," he told me. "It should be safe for you to sneak out."

I grabbed my coat from the closet and followed

him to the front door. "Take the stairs down to the eighteenth floor before you use the elevator," he advised me quietly as I put my boots back on. "Get out on the second floor and take the stairs to the ground floor. Do you think you can find the service entrance again?"

I nodded and tried to hide how nervous I was feeling. It was strange, but I felt more intimidated at the thought of running into the doorman than I did at encountering a demon. The hell spawn wouldn't even notice me, thanks to my bracelet, but the doorman would toss me out in a heartbeat. Worst case scenario, he might try to detain me and call the cops. The last thing I needed was to come to the notice of the police. They'd arrest me as soon as they learned who I was.

"Thank you for the bracelet and for letting me see your home," I said and gave him a last, lingering kiss.

"Thank you for the necklace. Maybe one day, I'll be able to visit you wherever you live."

That wasn't likely to happen, so I merely smiled and didn't say anything. Sam was the only one who knew I was dating Zach. I doubted the others would be very happy if they found out that I was seeing someone.

He watched me until I reached the corner, then blew me a kiss before stepping back inside and closing the door. Retracing my route, I followed his instructions. To my horror, a familiar person was waiting on the second floor when the elevator door slid open. The white blond hair and frosty blue eyes belonged to Zach's bodyguard and chauffeur, Giles. At first, I thought I'd been busted, but he merely waited for me to step out. He gave me a cold look, but he didn't seem to recognize me. Luckily, he hadn't gotten a very good look at my face the first time I'd spoken to Zach outside his building.

With my heart beating hard and fast, I stepped around him and didn't look back as I headed down the hallway. Once I was around the corner, I ran to the stairs. I took them two at a time, silently praying that I wouldn't trip and draw unwanted attention. I slowed down at the bottom and opened the door a crack to peer outside. The hallway was empty, so I stepped out and scurried to the exit, donning my coat in the process.

Only when I'd left the safety of the building did I remember the feathered spy that had been watching me from the balcony across from Zach's bedroom. I tilted my head back, but I couldn't see all the way to the top of the building.

A bony hand came down on my shoulder and I yelped in surprise. Reaching for the dagger that was stashed inside a sheath in my pocket, I spun around to see Sam watching me in amusement. "I did not mean to startle you," he said contritely at my glare.

"Have you seen the raven? It was watching me from that building." I pointed up at the structure.

Alarmed, he searched for the bird, but couldn't spot it. "I do not see it, but that does not mean it is not watching us right now. We should head back to the store. It would appear that the storm has finally arrived."

I hadn't even noticed that the snow was falling much harder now. The sidewalk was completely covered and had become slippery and dangerous. It was going to be even more difficult to spot the skeletal bird if it was trailing us in this weather.

Linking arms in an attempt not to slip and fall in the ice, we hurried back towards Midtown. We only made it a couple of blocks before Nathan appeared in front of us. He hadn't bothered with a coat and his black sweater rapidly became dotted with white flakes. They settled in his hair, making him even more magically handsome. I felt guilty that I had such strong emotions for someone else when I was dating Zach. I wished I could drive the feelings that I had for Nathan away, but I couldn't control my heart. The only thing I could do was to try not to let it control me.

"Did you encounter any demons during your patrol?" he asked.

I shook my head and huddled deeper into my coat. The snow was now coming down so hard that I could barely see him even though he was standing only a few feet away. "We saw the raven, though. It hasn't attacked us yet, but it could be gathering a flock right now."

Taking my hint, he took our hands and zapped us all back to our lair.

It was far too warm inside to wear my coat. I shucked it off and stomped the snow off my boots on the mat next to the door. Sam copied me, then we toed our boots off and left them there to dry. We hung our coats up on hooks that had been added to the door. The heat would dry them soon enough.

"How did your patrol go?" Leo asked.

My face tried to flame bright red, but I managed to control it. The only patrolling I'd done had been related to running my hands all over Zach's body. I wasn't sure when he found the time to work out, but he had nicely defined muscles in his arms, chest, back and thighs. "It went fine," I replied. I took my seat at the table where a cup of tea and plate of cookies waited. Sophia nodded in acknowledgement of the grateful smile that I gave her.

Brie sat stiffly with her arms crossed. "Did you see the raven?"

"Yeah. It showed up, but it just watched us this time."

Sophia had a theory about that. "Animals can sense it when the weather is about to take a turn for the worse. I imagine most birds have found somewhere safe to roost. Perhaps it was not able to force them out of their nests to attack you this time."

I didn't think it had even tried to rally the troops, but I just shrugged. It had wanted me to know that it could find me whenever I wasn't in the store. Brie's spells kept the evil out and prevented demons from finding us, but her magic didn't seem to work against animals. I wondered how long it would be before the Hellmaster's pet bird narrowed down our location. This was the only safe haven we had in the city. If it was compromised, we would have to find somewhere else to hide.

Chapter Nine

Being stuck in limbo waiting to find the next portal to hell was boring beyond words. I had little to do in between my training sessions with Leo. There was only so much time I could spend in front of the TV before I would go insane. Sophia had cable TV, so there were plenty of shows for Sam to choose from. I just couldn't seem to become invested in any of the programs that he favored. They seemed petty and unimportant to me now that I was aware of the reality that few humans knew about.

A war had been raging between heaven and hell for thousands of years. It had all begun when Lucifer had rebelled and had risen up against God. The angel had managed to sway his followers into joining him. I wasn't sure how long their battle had lasted before God had kicked the rebels out.

They'd fallen from heaven and had entered hell. The demons weren't alone in the dismal dimension that acted as their prison. Human souls from unrepentant sinners had been waiting for them. Hell wasn't just a storage place for evil doers. It gave the demons something to do and a way for them to blow off steam from their confinement. Torturing the former humans was the main source of enjoyment they had. Gossiping was their second favorite form of entertainment.

Sitting on my bed, I was trying to read a book, but my eyes kept glazing over. Hearing soft footsteps approach, I looked up to see Sophia appear in the doorway. She was carrying a tray with a plate of sandwiches and the inevitable cup of tea. "I thought you might like some lunch," she offered.

Normally, I ate downstairs at the table. It was unusual for her to deliver my food to me and my eyes narrowed in suspicion. "What's going on?"

Placing the tray on the nightstand, she glanced at the doorway to make sure no one was in sight. "Nathanael and Briathos are arguing again."

I rolled my eyes. "Let me guess. They're talking about me." All arguments seemed to revolve around me these days.

Sighing heavily, she took a seat on the bed beside me. "They are just feeling restless. I am sure their altercation will blow over soon." The storm was so bad that not even the angels wanted to go out on patrol.

She showed no signs of wanting to return downstairs to listen to their nitpicking, so I asked her a question. "I read in one of your books that angels spend a lot of time honing their battle skills."

She inclined her head in agreement. "That is true."

"I guess they're gearing up for an all-out war with the demons."

"They were, but since the gates of heaven are now locked, it would seem that they will not be able to participate in the battles ahead."

"That really sucks," I said morosely. "I feel bad for them spending all that time becoming warriors for nothing. It seems like such a waste, since they've only fought with Lucifer and his minions when he tried to stage a hostile takeover." Most people called him Satan now, but either name seemed to apply to the Devil.

"That is not the only occasion when my brethren were called into battle," she said.

This was news to me. "Really? Who else have they fought?"

Contemplating whether to tell me or not, she reached her decision and leaned in close. I unconsciously leaned in as well as she spoke softly. "It is not widely known, but humans are not the only intelligent lifeforms in the universe."

I blinked at that, ready to smile at her joke. "Are you saying that aliens exist?"

"Yes."

Her blunt answer drove my smile away. "You mean

there really are little gray men with gigantic heads and big black eyes ready to invade our planet and probe us into submission?"

Her expression darkened. "The beings that we have encountered do not look the same way as humans imagine them to be," she said. "Some of these beings are benign, but others are very different. One species who discovered this world believed that they could use it for their entertainment. The other species was far more dangerous. Their intention was not to experiment, but to enslave. They were the first alien beings that we drove away."

"Who were they and when was this?"

"They called themselves Viltarans," she said and shuddered. "It was tens of thousands of years ago, when mankind had still been in its infancy."

"I guess it was so long ago that the aliens didn't make it into the history books."

"Writing had not been created back then," she confirmed. "The Viltarans sent out a pod that was designed to detect intelligent lifeforms. It landed on Earth and discovered humans, then sent back a signal to the mothership. They sent a small ship full of warriors who intended to transform people into their slaves using advanced technology."

I could just picture it; aliens with sophisticated weaponry versus humans with crude clubs and rocks. "What happened? How did you fight them off?"

"God's soldiers chose human hosts and fought the aliens in hand to hand combat." She wasn't a soldier and probably hadn't taken part in the battle, but she still smiled at the memory. "The Viltarans assumed the humans had access to magic when they conjured swords seemingly out of the air. They had no way of knowing that angels were controlling the humans and were healing their flesh when they became wounded. When it became obvious that their foes weren't going to be easy to subdue, the aliens gave up and fled to their ship."

"They haven't been back?"

"Not as yet."

"Who were the other aliens? Did they try to take us over, too?"

Her expression turned rueful. "No. Their purpose was very different from conquering us, although many women fell prey to their charms."

Thoroughly confused by her answer, I reached for my tea. "Who were they? What did they want?"

"They were called gods by the Norse people," she said with a sniff.

That rang a bell. "Wait a minute, are you talking about Thor, Odin and the others that I can't remember?"

"Yes." Her lips pressed together in a prim line. "They discovered our world and realized that humans did not possess magic or great strength as they did. They believed this made them superior to your kind."

"You can't really blame them," I said, hardly able to believe we were having this discussion. "Thor could call lightning from the sky, from what I've heard."

"He was one of the most arrogant of all the Asgardians," she said darkly. "The sheer number of women that he bedded was phenomenal."

I hid my snigger behind my cup and took a sip of tea. "He must have been pretty hot if so many women fell for him."

"He fathered many children in the time that he and his kind spent on this world." My mouth dropped open in shock at that. "Fortunately, none of the Asgardians passed their powers on to their offspring," she added.

"I thought they were just legends," I mused. "I can't believe there are actual humans with Asgardian genes running around."

"It is just as well that they were not able to spread their abilities to mankind."

"Why?" I could tell there was something troubling her.

"Not all of the Asgardians thought kindly of humans. One in particular hated your kind. He felt nothing but contempt for beings who were weak and pitiful in his eyes. His powers were dark and malevolent compared to his kin's. If he'd taken an interest in Earth women like Thor did and had managed to pass on his power to his progeny, the consequences would have been catastrophic."

A shiver went down my spine. "Who was he?"

"His name was Loki."

"I've heard of him. Isn't he the God of Mischief, or something like that?"

"He was," she confirmed.

"You're talking about them in the past tense," I noted. "Angels didn't kill them, did they?"

"No. They are still alive. We merely advised them that it was time for them to return to their own realm. Earth is not a plaything that they can visit and cause havoc whenever they please."

"How did the angels manage to convince them to leave?"

"Arrogantly believing that he was undefeatable, Thor issued a challenge to God's messengers. He told them that if anyone could best him in hand to hand combat, that they would return home and never bother us again. If he lost, Earth would remain as their playground indefinitely."

From her self-satisfied smile, and the fact that we weren't currently being ruled by the Asgardian race, I knew what the outcome had been. "Who took on that challenge?"

"One of the Seraphim. He was the greatest of God's warriors. He stepped forward to challenge Thor and won, of course. Not even an Asgardian can best a holy champion. They have their own form of honor and could not go back on their word. Consequently, they had no choice but to leave."

I noted that she'd said the Seraphim *had* been the greatest warrior, but something in her tone told me not to question her further about him. He must have fallen out of favor with their creator somehow. It made me sad to think that an angel who had been so high in God's army could have fallen so low.

Cocking her head to the side, tension eased out of her body as she listened to what was going on downstairs. "It appears that the arguing has stopped. Hopefully, the peace will last for more than five minutes this time."

"Thanks for bringing me my lunch," I said. "And for telling me that story."

"It was my pleasure." She smiled then left me alone to contemplate the legends that had actually been based on true events. I'd never heard of Viltarans before and was glad that they'd been banished long before my birth. I had my own battles with the armies of hell to face. Fighting a war against hostile aliens wasn't high on my list of things to do in my lifetime.

Chapter Ten

Thick snow continued to fall. It blanketed the entire city, clogging the roads and bringing traffic to a standstill. Two days later, I was tired of being cooped up inside and I was itching to escape.

Almost our entire group was gathered at the table. Sam was the only one missing. He was upstairs with his butt glued to the couch. Feeling restless, I left my seat and walked over to the front door. Shifting the purple curtain aside, I looked out through the window. The sidewalk in front of the store had disappeared beneath two feet of snow. Parked cars had become shapeless white lumps. The street hadn't been plowed yet and the asphalt was completely hidden.

"Have you ever seen it snow this bad in Manhattan before?" I said over my shoulder to Sophia.

She shook her head. "There have been other storms that nearly rivalled this during the past eighteen years, but this is the worst that I have ever seen."

It had finally stopped snowing sometime during the night. Clouds still hung low in the air, threatening to unleash more mayhem. There had been several deaths reported on the news. Most had been heart attacks. People just didn't seem to realize how much hard work was involved in shoveling snow. The victims had mostly been older people with heart conditions.

I wasn't the only one who was restless from our forced inactivity. Brie wore a perpetually sour look on her face. We were growing tired of walking on eggshells around each other and our tempers were growing shorter by the hour.

Sophia had stocked up on food before the storm had hit. She'd been practicing her cooking skills since she now had me to feed. A plate of homemade cookies sat on the table. They were oatmeal, which wasn't my favorite, but they were still pretty good. Even Sam had tried one and he hadn't barfed it back up afterwards.

The store was a small two story building, which meant I couldn't escape from Nathan's constant presence. I could feel him watching me whenever my back was turned. I caught the longing in his eyes several times and it sparked a corresponding wistfulness in me. In an ideal world, we could date freely and maybe even get married one day. Any children that might eventually come along would be normal, happy and healthy. But this wasn't an ideal world and that could never happen for us.

I was resigned to the fact that dating Nathan was a dream that would never come true. I was stuck with the reality that I would never be able to be with the man I truly loved. Zach made me feel things that I'd never felt before, but the demons inside me were partially responsible for that. If I ever managed to evict them from my head, there was a good chance that everything would change between us. My fiery passion could very well die once they were gone and our relationship might die along with it. I shuddered at the thought that Zach might one day discover the true cause of my lust for him. He'd run screaming if he knew that I was harboring so many evil beings inside me.

Having feelings for two different guys was something I wouldn't wish on anyone. I wouldn't even wish it on Brie, not that she could ever suffer from anything as mundane as actual human emotions. She might have taken possession of a girl's body, but she was all self-righteous angel inside.

"What are you thinking about?" Leo asked. He'd left his seat and was standing behind me. He could see my morose expression in my reflection in the window.

I couldn't very well tell him the truth. Some thoughts were just too private to share. An idea popped into my head and I voiced it. "I was thinking about how bored I am. An epic snow fight might be in order now that it's finally stopped snowing."

Brie turned to face us. Unsurprisingly, her upper lip was curled derisively. "What an utterly childish and pointless idea."

"I think it will be fun," Leo said. His eyes were bright at the prospect of action that didn't involve stabbing someone with a blunt stick while training. He was far more willing to try new things than his twin was.

"I agree," Nathan said. "It will be good for us all to leave the confines of this building for a while."

Sophia sent him a startled look. "Surely you do not think that I will be joining you in this game?"

"Of course you will," I said with growing enthusiasm. I'd never been in a snow fight before. The closest I'd ever come was being pelted by my classmates while I'd run for my life after school. It had all been part of the fun of being the weird loner who preferred to sit alone and read than to communicate with other people. "Sam!" I shouted. "Get down here!"

His feet thumped on the floor as he leapt off the couch. I followed his progress down the hall and then the stairs. He burst into the room holding a steak knife in his hand, wild eyed with fear. He frowned when he didn't see any danger. "What is wrong?"

"Nothing's wrong. We're all going out for a while. Grab your snow gear," I ordered. They stared at me in bemusement and I clapped my hands twice to get them all moving. "Now, people!" They didn't really need to be rugged up, but they would be noticed if they didn't dress appropriately. Brie grumbled, but dutifully teleported herself upstairs. Sophia, Nathan and Brie now shared a closet. I shared mine with Leo and Sam.

When we were all suitably dressed in warm gear, Nathan teleported us to one of the parks in the city. It was so deeply covered in snow that it was impossible to be able to tell which one it was. The city that was slowly becoming familiar to me looked completely different now.

"Split up and prepare for combat," I ordered. We scattered to the edges of the small park and formed a rough circle facing each other.

I built a low wall to crouch behind, then quickly gathered up snowballs. They were lined up side by side, waiting to be launched at my enemies. I knew exactly who I was going to target first.

Brie hadn't made a wall to hide behind. Her arsenal of icy projectiles was laughably pitiful. Sam had picked a spot to my right. I caught his eye and subtly nodded towards Brie. He smiled mischievously and picked up a snowball. Leo had set up to my left. Nathan was directly across from me. Brie was between Leo and Nathan and Sophia was between Nathan and Sam.

It was only sporting to give them some warning before opening fire. "Game on!" I yelled, then hurled the first snowball. Sam threw his a moment later.

Startled by my shout, Brie looked up just in time for both missiles to hit her in the face.

Leo giggled helplessly at his twin's surprised expression. His snowball fell out of his hand and disintegrated on the ground. Sophia lobbed a missile at Sam and he ducked under it. His projectile was more accurate and hit her in the chest. Her eyes narrowed and then the battle was on.

Laughing so hard that I could barely see, I didn't dodge quickly enough when I saw something come flying at me. Brie's missile hit me squarely in the side of my head. Her teeth were bared in a fierce grin as she scooped up more ammunition. She was having fun despite her determination to be surly. The snow fight was bringing out her competitive edge. I acknowledged her with a nod, knowing she could have thrown it a lot harder than that. She was getting into the spirit of things rather than using the battle as a chance to humiliate me further.

Snowballs flew thick and fast as we chose our targets at random. Sophia was surprisingly accurate. She wore a determined expression as she lobbed her projectiles at us. Aiming in my direction, alarm stole over her as she focused on something behind me.

Spinning around, I saw a black object arrowing towards my face. My eyes focused on it to see it was the undead raven. It was coming for me with its talons outstretched and triumph blazing in its single milky eye.

Throwing myself backwards, I landed in the snow

and put my arms up to protect my face. I watched through a slender gap as the bird opened its beak to utter a caw that never came. A snowball slammed into it, knocking it off its trajectory a moment before it could swoop down and gore me.

I tilted my head backwards to see an upside down Nathan striding towards me. He wore murder on his face and he had an armful of missiles. Another snowball flew at the bird when it made another attempt to attack me, this time it came from Brie. She bent to scoop up more snow, then let it fly. Leo, Sam and Sophia joined them, advancing on the bird as it tried to attack me again. Hit from five different directions, it croaked in frustration as its efforts to maul me were denied. With a final glare, it spun around and rapidly flapped away.

"That raven is very determined to cause you harm," Leo said uneasily when it was gone.

I was pretty sure it wanted to get its talons on me again. It was trying to forge another link between myself and its master, but I kept the thought to myself. Only Sophia, Sam and I knew about the reading that she'd performed for me. The messages that she'd received had been too disturbing to share with the others. Apparently, someone close to me was going to betray me. I just didn't know who it would be, or when it would happen.

Nathan offered me his hand and hauled me to my feet. He brushed the snow out of my hair with a tenderness that made my heart ache in longing.

"We should kill it," Sam suggested. He stared in the direction that the raven had disappeared in with a dark look.

"It is already dead," Brie pointed out. "What makes you believe that it can be killed?"

"Violet took its eye. If it can be hurt, it can be killed."

"I don't know if it can die when it's here," I said. "I can only kill demons when I'm in hell."

"That thing is not a demon," Brie said flatly. "It is merely a corpse that is inhabited by evil."

I didn't want to say it out loud, but the raven was almost the bird equivalent of Sam. He'd been taken to hell as a living human being. Over the centuries, his soul had become entwined with his body. He hadn't died like the raven, but had become a twisted replica of a man.

It wasn't just in this dimension that the bird could follow me. It could also track me down when I was in the shadowlands and in hell. If I had the chance, I would do my best to slay the raven once and for all.

Chapter Eleven

Snowplows were out in force by late that afternoon. They acted swiftly to clear the streets to enable traffic to flow again. The number of murders had slowed down during the past few days and people were starting to brave the sidewalks again. I didn't know why the demons had stopped their infighting, but I was glad to have a reprieve from the influx of souls. Maybe their master was aware that his minions were culling their rivals and had put a stop to it. He'd need all the soldiers he could muster to take over the entire world.

Since the sidewalks were now clear, there was no reason for me to stay cooped up inside. Our snow fight had unleashed my need for action. Leo was sitting across from me at the table and I directed a question at him. "Do you want to go out on a patrol?"

He was on his feet almost before I finished asking the question. "I thought you would never ask," he replied with a grin.

Sophia opened her mouth to say something, but I cut her off before she could issue her warning. "I know. You want us to wear warm clothes and to try to stay safe, right?"

"Right," she agreed with a smile. "I would be very upset if anything were to happen to either of you."

"We will be fine," Leo reassured her as we grabbed our coats from the back of the door. We donned them, then trooped out. He waited until we were a few blocks away, then checked to make sure we hadn't been followed by any of our friends. "I must confess, it is good to get away from Brie for a short while," he said.

I smirked in sympathy. "I take it she's getting on your nerves, too?"

He nodded morosely. "Whenever you are not within earshot, she harps on about you incessantly."

It didn't really surprise me, but I did feel a small stab of hurt that she disliked me so intensely. "What does she say?"

"She believes that you know where a portal to the seventh realm of hell is. She seems to think that you are delaying the inevitable and are deliberately putting the inhabitants of Earth in danger."

My mouth dropped open in outrage at that accusation. Sure, I'd put off going to hell the last time, but only because I wanted to meet up with Zach before risking my life again. Besides, I'd only delayed the trip for a few days. "That isn't true!" I said in self-defense. "I have no idea where a portal to the seventh realm is hidden!"

"I believe you," he said solemnly. "We are all just getting frustrated that it is taking so long for us to find it."

"I suppose everyone expects me to kill the remaining seven princes and find the rest of the pieces of the mystery object in a single weekend," I said with more bitterness than I'd realized I was harboring. A lot of pressure was riding on me. I felt weighed down by it and was frankly a bit resentful. This was exactly why I snuck off to meet Zach whenever I could. My life couldn't be about saving the world all the time. I needed some time for myself, too.

"Maybe not in one weekend," he said with a grin. "We just did not realize that it would take so much time to locate a portal to each of the different realms."

"Have you considered the possibility that it's supposed to take me this long to find them?" He looked startled by that prospect. "Fate shows me the next step when I need to know it, not beforehand."

The notion had just come to me out of the blue, but it made him thoughtful. "You could be right," he agreed. "Sophia only receives her visions when something of importance happens, or is about to happen. She cannot force them to come to her ahead of time."

Scanning the street constantly for the raven and for any other threats, I realized we were nearing the entrance to the portal where we'd first encountered Sam. To anyone but me, and probably demons, the entrance was hidden behind a brick wall. A tattered poster marked the spot where the doorway was.

I could see through the illusion to the dark alleyway that led to the shadowlands beyond. It was the only passageway that wasn't blocked by the wards that surrounded the city. Or it had been before I'd unlocked two more of them. Our enemies didn't know where the unlocked portals were yet. Even if they did stumble across them, they'd have to conquer the hellgates in the shadowlands before they'd be able to use them to get into hell.

Just as we reached the passageway, a demon captain and his five lackeys appeared out of thin air. They weren't alone. Each one had a struggling human in their grip. Grabbing Leo's hand, I pulled him into a doorway and nodded at the group. "A pack of demons just arrived."

He turned in time to see the captives being forced through the illusion of a wall. They disappeared from sight as they moved into the dimness beyond.

Both demons and angels had the same ability to teleport without being noticed. Now that I thought about it, that didn't seem to be the case for me. I could always see my friends and enemies whenever they came and went. I put it down to my general strangeness and apparently being somehow different from everyone else on the planet.

"Perhaps they are taking them to hell to become imps," Leo said grimly. "It is possible they have displeased the captain and he is planning on punishing them for their transgressions."

I had a really bad feeling about this. "I don't think so. I think they have something else in mind. Let's wait for a few minutes and see what happens."

We settled down to wait and only five minutes passed before they returned.

When they stepped out through the seemingly solid wall, the captives had become vessels for six more demons. Their faces flickered constantly, changing from normal, to hideous, then back again. One of them had stubby horns growing from her forehead that indicated she was a captain. They split into two groups and headed in opposite directions.

Leo couldn't see their true faces like I could, but his bracelet enabled him to see a faint red glow around their forms. The stronger the demon, the more intense their aura was. "It seems you were right," he said. "They have subverted the humans to their will."

"What do you think we should do? Follow them, or head back to the store?" We hadn't been gone for very long and I didn't relish the idea of returning already.

He was undecided for a moment, then reached a decision. "We should follow one of the groups to see where they are hiding." They'd gone underground and it was rare to see them emerge out into the open these days.

With that decision made, we hurried after the closest pack. At least we knew how fresh troops were entering the city now. If they came through as pure souls and went in search of a vessel, they were instantly drawn to me.

Someone had been clever enough to think of a way around that. They were forcing humans to enter the shadowlands where it seemed they could become possessed just like they were here on Earth. It probably only worked when they were on the border between our world and the shadowlands. That was roughly halfway along the passageway, judging by the story that Sam had told us about the captain who had taken him to hell. He'd evicted himself from the body and had killed the vessel rather than allowing him to return to Earth. The reverse had happened to these poor humans, but the principle was the same.

Chapter Twelve

We trailed after the demons at a safe distance. They didn't give any indication that they knew they were being followed. When they turned a corner, we hurried to catch up to them before they could disappear. I caught sight of them as they headed into an underground parking lot.

Crossing the street, we crept over to the lot. We peered through the entrance and watched as they took the long ramp downwards. A demon rune had been painted just inside the entryway. It was only faint at the moment and Leo probably couldn't even see it. The blood had dried, which meant it wasn't a fresh symbol. It would only become active once a demon put its bloody flesh on it. It was the same rune that had trapped us both before and I wasn't about to fall for that trick again.

Leo turned to say something and his eyes widened. I saw the raven reflected in his pupils a moment before it slammed into my back. It hit me so hard that I staggered forward into the trap. The demons had almost been out of sight when they sensed an alarm being triggered. The symbol on the wall was now glowing faintly. Turning, they started running back towards us. One of them would have to activate the rune in order to trap us inside the garage.

Spinning around to face the raven, I managed to raise my hands just in time to save my eyes from being punctured when it came at my face. Its beak tore at my fingers, trying to get at the soft orbs beneath them. Sam was right, it wanted revenge on me for taking its eye.

Leo didn't hesitate to think about the danger he was putting himself in and leaped into the parking lot after me. Grasping the bird by the wings, he tore it off me. I pulled my dagger out of my pocket and the crimson glow flared to life. The raven cawed in rage and flapped towards me again. I fended it off and glanced over my shoulder to see the demons closing in on us. We'd drawn their direct attention, which had the nasty side-effect of nullifying Brie's spell that hid us.

"It is Hellscourge!" one of them shouted when she recognized me. Teleporting to the entryway, she sliced her hand open and slapped her bleeding palm on the rune. It blazed to life and the trap sprang shut.

Conjuring up his sword, Leo slashed at the raven. It

managed to twist itself in midair and the blade narrowly missed slicing its head off. It let out a croak of laughter, then flew through the exit. Landing in a tree across the street, the raven perched on a thin branch. It settled in to watch the battle that we were about to become embroiled in. The trap had no effect on it at all, but we wouldn't be able to travel through the invisible barrier quite as easily. We would have to deactivate it before we would be able to leave.

We were surrounded by five lesser demons and their captain, but I wasn't particularly worried. We'd faced worse odds than this and had lived to tell the tale. I shucked off my heavy coat so it wouldn't restrict my movements. I wished I had the same strength and skill that I could call on in the shadowlands and in hell, but here I was just a frail human. My legion gave me some extra power when I was in this dimension, but not much.

"Well, well," the captain drawled. "Look what the raven dragged in." He smirked as he circled us. Leo and I stood back to back, waiting for them to attack, as we knew they would. "It was very stupid of you to allow yourself to be led into our trap."

"Can we just get on with it?" I said in a mocking tone. "Do we have to listen to your pathetic attempts to gloat first?"

His face darkened at the insult and he made his glowing red sword appear. "Have it your way then. Dispatch the angel's vessel," he told his minions. "Then we will take the girl before our master."

Neither Leo, nor I were willing to go along with his plan. Thanks to the training the twins had instilled in me, I was able to hold my own in battle now. I still became tired far more quickly than my foes, but at least I was no longer helpless.

Leo was shorter than me, but he was a skilled warrior. His experience in battle made up for his small size and he took down two of the lesser demons easily. Our enemies didn't believe in fighting fair. I was trying to fend off the captain as well as two of his minions. They were doing their best to disarm me without harming me too badly. At least there were still some hell spawn who weren't trying to kill me outright. Some preferred to try to take me into their custody so they could receive a reward from the Hellmaster.

Leo cut down another lackey and I managed to stab the captain in the heart. Together, my young friend and I finished off the final minion.

"Well, that was easy," Leo said and his sword disappeared.

I was too busy absorbing their displaced souls to answer him. I concentrated hard, but didn't pick up any clues from the barrage of memories that I received. When my vision cleared, I shook my head at his unspoken question. "They didn't give me anything new to go on."

"Perhaps you will learn something next time," he said with a shrug. We'd reached the stage where ejecting demons from their vessels so I could absorb them was now commonplace for us.

We turned towards the exit just as something materialized right in front of me. Vaguely humanoid, the figure seemed to be made of living shadows. It was around seven feet tall, and evil emanated from it so thickly that it was hard to catch my breath. A sword appeared in its hand. Instead of glowing red, the blade was dead black. It was also made of living shadows. It was like a humanoid version of one of the nightmares that drew my carriage when I was in hell. The only difference was that its eyes were black rather than crimson. That was if it had eyes at all. I couldn't make out any features in its misty face.

"My master has a message for you, Hellscourge," it intoned in a deep, hollow voice that was distinctly masculine. I changed the gender from 'it' to 'he' in my mind.

"I can't wait to hear this," I said, trying to hide my trepidation behind a flippant tone. "Lay it on me."

"Stay out of his realm, or suffer the consequences," he warned me. He moved so quickly that I barely managed to react in time when he thrust his sword at me. I tried to deflect it with my own blade, but his weapon passed straight through it. Piercing my stomach, the shadowy metal turned solid. The creature wrenched the blade sideways and hot pain flooded through me. Finished with his task of slicing me open, he faded, then dissipated to nothingness. His hollow chuckle lingered in the air.

Chapter Thirteen

In too much pain to voice my screams, I fell to my knees, trying to hold my intestines inside my body. Leo let out a cry of horror as blood sheeted out of me. He grabbed me by the shoulder and tried to teleport me to safety, but we were still caught in the demons' trap. "This is going to hurt," he warned me, "but I have no choice."

He hauled me to my feet and I groaned in agony. I came close to passing out when he pulled my arm over his shoulder. He dragged me over to the rune and took hold of my hand that was still clutching my dagger. Holding my hand so only I had contact with the weapon, he scraped the blade across the symbol to deactivate it. The glow flickered and died, releasing us from our imprisonment. Bending to grab my coat, he zapped us back to our lair.

"Nathan!" he shouted as soon as we appeared in my bedroom. He sat me down on my bed, then lifted my feet up so I could lie down. I curled on my side, still trying to keep my guts from sliding out onto the floor.

My guardian materialized a moment later. Taking in the blood that was draining out of me, he pushed Leo towards the door. With a final worried look over his shoulder, the teen left, closing the door behind him.

Nathan dropped to his knees beside me. His expression was intent and anguished as he looked into my eyes. "You know what I have to do," he said in a low voice.

It would be dangerous for him, but I would die if he didn't heal me. I managed a pained nod of acknowledgement that doubled as permission. Sliding a hand behind my head, his fingers became tangled in my hair as he bent to kiss me.

The moment our lips touched, the pain faded and bliss swelled inside me. It took longer than usual for it to spread throughout my body. My wound was so terrible that it wasn't easy to heal. Then my flesh knitted back together and I was suddenly bursting with his holy essence. Filled with strength, I pulled him onto the bed. He lay sprawled on top of me, chest to chest as we kissed like our lives depended on it. Our groins were also pressed together. I felt him react to my nearness, proving that his vessel was a healthy young male who felt lust just like any normal human.

My hands were sliding down his back towards his butt when the door burst open. Neither of us cared that we had an audience. Our hungry mouths devoured each other and we both fought it as he was torn away from me. We reached for each other, but Brie and Leo dragged him away while Sam and Sophia pinned me to the bed. The angels disappeared as they teleported somewhere else. I went limp when the connection to my guardian was severed.

Dizzy and reeling, I shook my head. "What just happened?" I asked. I remembered grabbing Nathan's butt and my face tried to flame in embarrassment.

"That was a very close call," Sophia replied. She and Sam cautiously released me and helped me to sit up.

"What was? What did I do?"

"You were ravishing Nathanael," Sam told me. He meant it as a joke, but it hit me like a bucket of cold water to the face. I had very nearly despoiled a being that was very close to perfect.

Rubbing my face with both hands, I looked at Sophia. "We can't let that happen again."

"I agree," she said solemnly. "Unfortunately, it was necessary this time. If he had not used his grace to heal you, you would have died." She gestured at the blood that soaked the bed and the carpet.

"What happened?" Sam asked.

"It was all the raven's fault," I said darkly. My body was starting to feel the effects of Nathan's infusion and I bounced to my feet. "Leo and I followed a pack of demons to their base, then the raven pushed me into a trap. We killed the captain and his minions, then something else appeared."

"What was it?" Sophia asked.

I described it and her face went pale. "Oh dear," she said in a faint voice. "The Demon Princes are getting desperate indeed if they are resorting to these measures."

"What was that thing?" I asked.

"I have heard that they are the embodiment of evil and that they are impossible to kill."

"How am I supposed to defeat it then?" Pacing up and down, my frustration was high.

"That I do not know. Any one of the Princes could be responsible for unleashing it upon you."

"Great," I said and threw my hands in the air. "I still have seven of them to whittle down. He could send his creature after me anytime."

"I think not," she refuted. "He only appeared after the trap was triggered. As long as you remain unnoticed, he will hopefully be unable to locate you."

Feeling surly, I knew I was pouting like a child. My body yearned for Nathan to finish what we'd started. The lust that I felt with Zach was nothing next to the need that was inside me right now. I felt as if a part of me had been torn away and that I'd never be whole again unless we were together.

"Are you feeling all right?" Sam asked. He wore an uneasy frown as he watched me pace up and down.

"No. I feel strange." The energy was growing inside

me until I thought I would burst from it. Sophia caught my eye and gave a soft gasp. "What?" I asked.

"Your eyes are glowing," she said in awed wonder.

Freezing for a moment, I raced down the hall and into the bathroom. Instead of glowing crimson, my eyes were blazing with blue light. "What the hell?" I said in confusion.

Leo appeared beside me just as Sam entered the room. Taking in my eyes, Leo grabbed us both and teleported us to a rooftop somewhere in the city. Bending down, he tore a large sheet of plastic off the ground, then gave me a hard shove.

Pin-wheeling my arms for balance, I fell backwards and landed in water. It was shockingly cold and I sucked in a breath. Water filled my lungs and I thrashed my arms and legs until I reached the surface. Coughing up liquid that tasted of chlorine, I swam towards the ladder, but Leo barred my way. "You have ingested too much of Nathan's grace," he informed me. "Swimming in near freezing water should be an expedient way to burn it off."

"I hate you so much right now," I said with chattering teeth. Sam's lips quivered, then he let out a snigger at my pitiful tone. "I hate you, too," I snarled.

At the imp's wounded look, Leo put his arm around his shoulder. "You do not hate either of us. You love us and you will prove it by doing what I ask."

Muttering beneath my breath, I knew he was right and started swimming. I was infused with far too much energy. It would be dangerous to allow it to grow. I had to get rid of it somehow and this was as good a way as any.

Chapter Fourteen

Just as Leo had planned, the combination of frigid water and exercise did the trick of sapping away my extra energy. I managed to catch glimpses of the rooftop as I swam up and down the long, narrow pool. Most of the furniture lay beneath plastic covers. Snow was heaped right up to the edge of the waist high glass walls that surrounded us on three sides. I spied a door that led deeper into the building near the shallow end of the pool. The snow wasn't as deep there. It looked like someone periodically exited through the door to clear the path.

Leo crouched down when I reached the end where he was waiting. "Your eyes have stopped glowing," he told me. "How do you feel?"

"I'm starting to get tired. Apart from that, I feel okay."

He debated about it, then offered me his hand. "You can get out now."

"Gee, thanks," I said dryly. He hauled me out effortlessly and I walked over to join Sam. He'd waded through the snow over to the balcony, leaving a deep pathway that I followed. He was staring at the city, mesmerized by the view. If it had been nighttime, it would have been even more spectacular.

I used my hands and legs to push the snow away so I could stand beside him. "Who does this building belong to?" I asked Leo when he carved out a spot on Sam's other side.

He leaned his elbows against the wall, not at all bothered that he was standing waist deep in snow. The cold didn't affect me as much as it had before I'd become a receptacle for evil souls, but I was dripping wet and started to shiver. He shrugged at my question. "I have no idea. I spied this pool during one of my patrols and thought it might be of use to us in an emergency."

Sam slanted a look at him. "You knew that Violet and Nathan would require your intervention?"

"Sophia warned us that it could become necessary."

I grimaced at that, wishing she'd given me the same warning. "Do you know what that thing was that stabbed me?"

He shook his head. "I have never seen anything like it before."

"I think it was a Wraith Warrior," Sam offered.

"That sounds ominous," I said. "What do you

know about them?"

"Not much. I have heard that they are only used very rarely," the imp said. "They are the Princes' personal assassins. It is rumored that they are conjured up from their unholy essence."

"How can we defeat him if he's made of demon essence?"

Sam's expression was solemn. "I do not think he can be defeated. He will remain in existence until the Prince merges his minion back inside him, or so I have heard."

"They must be very afraid if they are going to such lengths to try to frighten you away," Leo mused. "How is your wound now?"

"It's gone," I replied and lifted my shirt to show him.

His grin dropped away at whatever he saw. Sam blanched in horror. With dread, I looked down to see what they were staring at. Instead of unblemished skin, I had a ten-inch scar running across my abdomen. Black tendrils spread outwards from the necrotic looking edges.

Feeling faint, I staggered backwards in a futile effort to escape from my own body. Sam and Leo caught me before I could flounder deeper into the snow.

"The others need to see this," Leo decided. Before I could form a protest, he waved a hand over me to instantly dry me off, then teleported us back to our base.

Brie had returned with Nathan sometime during our absence. They were sitting at the table with Sophia. All three of them looked at us when they realized that we had appeared. Nathan was pale and haggard. Forgetting my own problems, I hurried towards him. Brie left her seat to intercept me. "That is close enough," she said, barring my way when I was still two yards away from him. She was glaring at me as if I was a cockroach that she wanted to squish beneath her heel.

"What's wrong with him?" I asked.

"*You* are what is wrong with him," she replied icily. "Every time he heals you, he gives up a part of himself. This time, you nearly drained him of his essence."

Appalled by that prospect, I met his eyes. "Is that true?"

Dropping his gaze to the tabletop, he refused to answer me, so I turned to Sophia. "How close did I come to stealing his grace?" I hadn't even known it was possible to do so, but I could see the evidence sitting right in front of me.

"Perilously close," Sophia replied. "If we had not separated you when we did, there is a very good chance that he would have become like me."

My eyes filled with tears of remorse and self-loathing. I loved him more than anyone else on the planet and I'd nearly destroyed what made him so perfect.

"Do not blame yourself," Nathan said hoarsely. "I

gave you my essence of my own free will."

Brie sneered, but her ire was aimed at me rather than him. "You have lost the ability to be objective when dealing with Violet. You have no free will when it comes to her. She has bewitched you."

I knew she disliked me, but calling me a witch was taking things a bit too far. "You're the one who casts spells," I reminded her. "If I'm a witch, what the hell does that make you?"

"What do you think you are doing when you use demon runes?" she said archly. "I use my holy grace to cast my spells. Tell me," she eyed me in distaste, "what type of power do you think it is that *you* use?"

We all knew the answer to that and I fell silent. The demons inside me gave me the only power I had. Without them, I was as helpless as any normal human.

"You need to show them what has happened to you," Leo said, reminding me of why we'd rushed back here. I wasn't looking forward to revealing this development. Brie would no doubt take it as further proof that I was evil to the core.

"Show us what?" she said suspiciously.

My answer was to lift my shirt up to reveal the ugly black scar. She recoiled as if finding out that I had the plague. In a way, I did. I carried something horrible inside me and I didn't know what it was yet.

Nathan sucked in a breath and dread filled his face. "The being that attacked you was a Wraith Warrior?" he asked.

I nodded and dropped my shirt. My number of scars was growing and they were getting uglier each time. "He was sent by a Prince. I don't know which one it was yet." Silence reigned and I sensed that they wanted to have a discussion without me listening in. "I'm going to take a shower." Sam followed me into the kitchen and the others started whispering even before we'd reached the stairs.

Following me into my room, Sam hovered there uncertainly while I gathered some fresh clothes. "I know it looks bad, but I am sure that you will be okay," he said with as much confidence as he could muster.

"Will I?" I asked softly. Somehow, I doubted that I would ever be okay again. He dropped his eyes and his posture slumped in defeat. I hated to cause him more misery, so I bumped my shoulder against his. "Is there anything good coming on TV?"

He brightened at my attempt to cheer him up. Glancing at my watch, he nodded. "One of my favorite shows will be starting in fifteen minutes."

"I'd better hurry then," I said with a forced grin. I headed for the bathroom and tried not to look at the mark that stretched across my abdomen as I showered. I could almost feel the evil insidiously spreading through me. Glancing down when I'd dried myself off, I blanched when I saw that the tendrils that emanated from the scar were slowly moving.

It took a couple of minutes before the color returned to my face. I was almost back to normal by the time I took a seat on the couch next to Sam. He didn't question me when I sat close enough for our knees to touch. He simply put his arm around my shoulder and pulled me in closer. He pretended not to notice when I wiped my tears away with my sleeve.

Chapter Fifteen

I lay awake when I went to bed. Staring up at the ceiling, I brooded about the future. Sam was across the hall, watching TV with the volume turned down low. The others were still downstairs. They were most likely discussing our options, not that we had many.

I let out a shuddering sigh, willing my tears away. Nathan had saved me from death dozens of times and in repayment, I'd almost drained him of his grace. The thought of making him less than the majestic being that he was filled me with horror. Sophia was only a shell of who she'd once been, thanks to the demons stripping her holy essence away. Most of her power was gone and she'd only been left with a touch of clairvoyance.

Despair overwhelmed me. It clung to me like a stench that I couldn't get rid of when I finally drifted off to sleep. I was drawn to the shadowlands inside my mind where the legion was waiting for me.

Morax studied me when I appeared before him. "You seem different," he said in his guttural voice. Lesser demons were ugly, but he and his fellow Demon Lords were even more hideous than their minions. They stood head and shoulders above all but the captains, who were half a foot or so shorter than them.

"I ran into a Wraith Warrior," I said despondently. "Or into his sword, to be more precise."

Shocked breaths were drawn in and my hand strayed to my midsection involuntarily. Morax reached out and yanked my jacket up to reveal the new black scar. "He marked you," he said in a strangled tone.

He'd done more than mark me, he'd scrambled my insides as well. "Gee, what gave it away?" I said sarcastically and stepped back out of his reach. I'd dreamed myself to be wearing my favorite black jacket with the skull buckles and a pair of ratty blue jeans with a few too many holes.

"You do not understand what this means." His tone and expression were ominous as whispers swept through the crowd. Gossip was already spreading to everyone who was standing too far away to hear us.

I learned firsthand how annoying it was to be left hanging when he didn't continue. It was no wonder Brie always got so annoyed when I did this to her. "Spill it," I ordered.

"No matter how powerful a demon is, a wound from a Wraith Warrior means instant banishment back to the first realm of hell. Marking a living being such as you can have only one outcome." He let the tension build before he finished. "Death." He drew the word out dramatically.

"Wow, don't sugarcoat it for me or anything," I said, trying to hide the flutter of terror that rose inside me.

He staunchly ignored my sarcasm and his gaze went distant as he looked through me rather than at me. "I sense that you have been infected with evil. It is likely to spread through you until your insides rot and become putrid. I am amazed that you are still alive."

I heaved a deep sigh that travelled all the way up from my toes. Nathan's infusion of grace had slowed the process, but it hadn't stopped it completely. Maybe I wouldn't have to worry about the Wraith Warrior turning up again. One stab was apparently enough to kill me. Then again, the shadowy being had already guessed that I wouldn't die straight away. Why else would he have warned me to stay away from his master? "Is there a cure for this sort of wound?"

Morax looked at me pityingly. "Only the Prince who sent the assassin after you would have the capacity to undo this dark spell. Considering that they all want you dead, it is highly unlikely that the one who is responsible will agree to do so."

"You're just full of good news, aren't you?" He was

used to my snarky attitude by now and took no offence. "Do any of the new arrivals know where a portal to the seventh realm of hell is?" I was pretty sure I already knew the answer, but I had to ask.

Glances were exchanged and Morax shook his head. "No. We are as in the dark as you are."

"Great. I guess I'll just slowly rot and die and take you all down with me then." They blanched at my malicious remark. Ignoring them, I turned on my heel and stomped over to the house that I'd created for Heather.

She opened the door before I could knock and ushered me inside. "Hi," she said brightly. Shifting her weight from foot to foot, she fidgeted nervously.

"Hi." I eyed her as she wrung her hands together. "What's wrong?"

"Nothing!" Her eyes cut to the side, a sure sign that she was lying. With her blond hair and green eyes, we looked enough alike that we could have been sisters.

Spying movement behind the couch, I narrowed my eyes in suspicion. "Are you hiding someone in here?" She didn't answer and I cast my memory back to the crowd outside. I belatedly realized that someone had been missing. "It's the scribe, isn't it?"

I heard a sigh, then he popped up from behind the couch. He was the only demon who wore a black robe. Now that he was busted, he slunk around the couch to join us.

"Don't be mad," Heather said in a forlorn voice. "It just gets so lonely being here all by myself. The other demons were picking on him, so I offered to let him stay here as long as he doesn't try anything funny."

"Has he tried anything funny?" I asked.

He sent me an indignant look. "I have no interest in a human," he said then sent Heather an almost apologetic look. "I mean no offense, of course."

"That's okay," she said. "I have no interest in you either."

I would have been very surprised if she had. A Demon Prince had defiled her and she'd bled to death in his bed. "I'm not mad at you," I said, to her surprise. "This is your house. You can invite anyone you like inside."

She shuddered at the thought of letting any of the other demons in. "I'm sure one is enough."

"How have you been?" I asked rather lamely. "Do you need anything?"

"I'm doing okay," she replied and cut a look at her companion. "Sy has a request, though."

"Sy?" I said blankly then realized she was talking about the scribe.

"My name is Sytry," he said. "Heather has shortened it to Sy."

He didn't seem particularly amused when I smirked. "You know us humans, we're always giving things nicknames." Heather smiled back at me. I was glad that she had someone to keep her company, even if it was one of the hell spawn. Sy was timid in comparison to the other demons. Like Sophia, he was more of a scholar than a warrior. "What do you need?" I asked him.

He ducked his head almost shyly, hesitant to make his request. Heather elbowed him in the side to prompt him to speak. "If it would not be too much trouble, I would really appreciate it if you would provide me with some sketchpads and pencils," he said at last.

His runes had come in handy a few times now. I didn't see any reason to deny him his request. I concentrated and a stack of sketchpads appeared on the dining table. A range of pencils materialized in a mug beside them. "The sketchpads and pencils will keep renewing themselves if you run out," I told him. Or so I hoped. I was still learning about what I could do with the construct that I'd made inside my own mind.

His crimson eyes lit up in happiness. "Thank you!" He rushed over to the table, took a seat and snatched up one of the pads as if expecting me to make them disappear again.

"That was really nice of you," Heather said to me softly. "You didn't have to do that."

"It didn't cost me anything," I shrugged.

Sneaking a look over her shoulder to make sure he wasn't listening to us, she leaned in close to whisper. "Now maybe I'll get a break from his non-stop gossiping."

We shared a hushed giggle and Sy looked around suspiciously before returning to his drawing. "Did he tell you anything interesting in his gossip?" I wasn't sure which realm he was from, but I knew that he'd lived in one of the palaces.

"Just a lot of bitching and moaning about how horrible demons are and how much they tease him for not being a warrior," she replied. "Nothing that will help you, I'm afraid."

I hoped someone would be able to shed some light on where the next portal was soon. I had even more reason to hurry now that I'd apparently been doomed to death by the Wraith Warrior's blade.

Chapter Sixteen

Several days passed with little of consequence happening. Nathan, Brie and Leo had resumed their patrols once the snow had been cleared. Leo took me with him a couple of times and I went out with Sam on the other days. I could no longer count on Brie to have my back and no one trusted me to be alone with Nathan. Not after I'd come so close to draining him of his grace.

We learned that the demons were back to eliminating their rivals when a pack of souls came knocking at the door, so to speak. Sophia discovered them when she opened the door to head outside for food. I was in the middle of training with Leo and turned when she sucked in a breath. The black demon essence tried to flow past her, but were repelled by Brie's spells.

Even in their pure spirit form, our enemies still couldn't enter our domain. It was disturbing that they'd tracked me here. It was lucky they hadn't been followed by curious demons. Then again, they tended to stay on their own turf rather than venturing out to explore. The evidence that rivals were often cut down was floating right in front of us. Humans weren't able to see them. Apparently, only those of us who had been exposed to the supernatural world could.

I knew they would find their way inside me the moment I left the safety of the store. There was no point in delaying the inevitable, so I might as well get it over with. Sophia shifted aside when I approached her. The moment I stepped outside, I was bombarded by souls. I braced myself for the inundation of memories when their oily, yet insubstantial essence boiled inside me.

Leo's expression was hopeful when I returned to train with him after the barrage ended. "Did you pick up anything from them?"

Well used to being invaded by now, I adjusted to the influx of a dozen new souls with barely a pause. "Nope. Just more mayhem and dismemberment stories to add to the collection." He shrugged philosophically and we resumed our mock fighting. The new arrivals had been two captains and ten lesser lackeys. They weren't high enough on the demon hierarchy to know anything that could help us.

Nathan was sitting at the table with Brie. His eyes were on me and it was all I could do not to stare at him in return. He'd finally regained his energy and was back to his usual strength again. He'd lost the haggard look that he'd gotten from having his essence depleted. It seemed that angels could replenish their grace as long as enough of it still remained inside them. If I'd taken even a little bit more, he would have become permanently depleted of his power.

"It is my turn to escort Violet on a patrol," Nathan said when Leo called a halt to our training session a couple of hours later.

Sophia had returned with the groceries and was in the kitchen making lunch for me. She paused what she was doing when Brie automatically protested. "It is too dangerous for you two to be alone together." The look she sent me was bordering on contemptuous. Upstairs, I could hear the TV going. Sam was no doubt glued to the screen in fascination. I wished he was here to back me up rather than watching one of his beloved shows.

"What do you think I'm going to do?" I demanded. "Drag Nathan off to a hotel to have my way with him and steal his grace in the process?" Having my way with him sounded pretty good, but stealing his essence, not so much.

"For all we know, that is exactly what you will do."

"We will leave once you have finished your lunch," Nathan said to me, ignoring the teen completely. She sent him a furious look, but Leo shook his head at her in warning. Nathan had made up his mind and he wasn't going to be dissuaded by anyone.

To be honest, I was dreading spending time alone with my guardian. I wasn't sure if I would be able to control myself if I was wounded and he had to heal me again.

Sophia entered the room carrying a tray with a sandwich for me and tea for both of us. "I have been thinking," she said as she took her seat. Leo handed me the plate and cup of tea. "I believe the only reason you drained so much of Nathan's grace was because of the wound that the Wraith Warrior inflicted on you."

Intrigued by her theory, I paused before I could take a bite out of my sandwich. "What do you mean?"

"I think that your body was trying to undo the new type of evil that had invaded you. You didn't ingest a soul that you could simply absorb this time. He infected you with something far worse than that. If Nathan had not given his grace to you, I am certain that you would have died."

"Yeah," I agreed. "That's pretty much what Morax said."

Nathan's brows rose to hear that news. "What did the Demon Lord say to you, exactly?"

"I can't remember his exact words," I replied. "It was something along the lines of I should have died immediately and he was surprised that I was still alive."

Even Brie looked unsettled by this. "Did he say anything else?" she asked.

"Only that the evil is going to spread through me,

rotting me from the inside, but I'm sure that doesn't bother you at all."

A gasp came from the doorway and I looked up to see Sam's stricken face. "Tell me that there is a way we can save you," he pleaded.

I hated to hurt him, but I didn't want to give him any false hope. I was already starting to feel the effects of the toxin. My face was paler than usual and my hair had lost some of its luster. "That's doubtful. He said that the Demon Prince who sent the Wraith Warrior after me is the only one who might be able to stop this. Since they all want me dead, getting him to reverse the spell would be wishful thinking."

Sam looked at Nathan, who was now as stricken as the imp. "My grace can heal you," he said.

I shook my head at his desperate offer. "You saved my life when you gave me so much of your grace, but it didn't cure me." The room went bleak and silent when I added, "I'm pretty sure nothing will be able to fix this."

"You cannot give up so easily," Brie said harshly. "The world needs you."

"I haven't given up," I corrected her. "I'm just telling you what I know." I bit into my sandwich and it didn't taste as good as usual.

"You are being awfully calm about this," Leo observed.

Swallowing down the bite, I shrugged one shoulder. "Gnashing my teeth and wailing in anguish won't change anything. I'd rather save my energy for taking down the spawn of hell."

Brie was staring at me as if she'd never seen me before. "You will still continue on your mission even though your death warrant has almost assuredly been signed?"

"Killing the Demon Princes and their master is what I'm destined to do. I'll wipe out as many of them as I can before I die."

It was hard to say whether Nathan or Sam were more affected by my calm statement. They shared a look that wordlessly conveyed their pain at the thought of losing me.

"We will not allow you to perish," Sophia said firmly, as if she could somehow reverse what had been done to me. "We will find a way to save you."

As if it would be that easy. "Good luck with that." I softened the sarcasm with a weak smile and concentrated on eating.

When I'd finished my meal, I retreated upstairs to the bathroom. I took the opportunity to check my cell phone for messages when I was done. Zach hadn't contacted me yet and I didn't want to look too clingy and text him first. My phone was always either on silent, or set to vibrate when a message came through. I didn't want the others to know that I had it. I wasn't ready for them to find out that I had a boyfriend yet.

Based on Hagith's and Orifiel's reactions to the fact that I was spending time with Zach, I was pretty sure my friends wouldn't be pleased to learn about him either. I could only imagine how badly Brie would take it.

My boots and coat were downstairs, so I trudged down to collect them. Nathan was waiting for me, wearing similar clothes. He didn't open the door and instead took my arm and teleported us to another location.

Patrolling for demons wasn't the only reason we searched the streets. It was our hope that I'd be able to spy another portal to the shadowlands. So far, that plan wasn't working. My faith that Fate was guiding my path was beginning to wither. Now that I knew I was doomed to rot from the inside, I wondered if she'd given up on me. Maybe she'd arranged for me to die so she could choose another champion.

I would never abandon one of my warriors, Fate said into my mind. I halted in shock that she was contacting me directly. *Do not lose your faith. Know that I am watching over you and that there is a way to cure you of your affliction. It will not be easy and you will fall into the depths of despair first, but you can survive this. I promise that your suffering will make you stronger in the end.*

"What is it?" Nathan asked anxiously.

"Fate just spoke to me," I said in wonder that was mixed with confusion.

"What did she say?"

"She said that there is a way to cure me and that I shouldn't give up hope. She didn't tell me what the cure was, though." I didn't tell him about the part where I'd fall into the depths of despair first. He was already suffering enough and I didn't want to make his anguish any worse.

His smile was beautiful enough to take my breath away. "If Fate has told you this, then there is indeed hope."

I became lost in his eyes and wasn't able to form a response. He was just as mesmerized as I was. We didn't even need to touch each other to fall beneath the spell that had been forged between us.

When hands grabbed hold of me, I snapped out of my daze, but it was already too late to escape. I saw Nathan's expression turn to alarm then I was whisked away to somewhere else.

Chapter Seventeen

Bright white light blinded me, so I knew it was angels rather than demons who were responsible for my abduction. My stone bracelet was roughly stripped off my wrist while I was trying to free myself. The hands released me and I spun around to confront my attackers.

I wasn't at all surprised to see Hagith and Orifiel standing in front of me. Both wore expressions that were a mixture of smug and disapproving. They were beautiful, as all angels appeared to me. Hagith was blond and blue eyed. Orifiel had light brown hair and brown eyes. Their suits were tailored and dark. Hagith wore her hair up in a severe bun that did nothing to diminish her beauty.

"We warned you not to allow yourself to become distracted from your task," Hag said in an ominous tone.

"Now we will have to punish you for disobeying us," Orifice added.

"I wasn't even with Zach," I said in exasperation.

"We are not talking about the human boy," Hagith said in contempt. "Your infraction this time is far worse. You have corrupted a holy being and we find your actions to be unacceptable."

Guilt flooded through me at her accusation. "I didn't mean to take so much of Nathan's grace. It was an accident. If he hadn't used his essence to heal me, I would have died."

Orifiel rolled his eyes. "It is so typical of a human to find any excuse to explain your failings."

"We do not want to hear your pitiful reasons for your selfish actions," Hagith said in contempt. "We will not allow Nathanael to sully himself with you again."

They advanced on me and I backed away, searching for escape. We were in an empty room that could have been in any building in the city. My back hit the wall and I had nowhere to go.

They each placed a hand on my head and pain erupted throughout my entire body. White hot holy fire burned me from my head to my toes. No part of me was safe from the invasion. Deep inside my mind, I heard the legion screaming in agony and realized that my voice had joined theirs. It only lasted for a few seconds, but it seemed to go on forever. Then the pain stopped abruptly and the angels stepped away from me.

"Now, perhaps you will do as we say in the future," Hag said primly. Her expression was grave, but I saw glee dancing in her eyes. She wiped her hand on her skirt, as if trying to rid herself of my evil after touching me.

Orifice was wearing a slight grimace, as if he hadn't enjoyed the torture as much as his partner had. He took my bracelet out of his pocket and dropped it at my feet. "We will be watching you," he warned me, then they both disappeared.

Panting in the aftermath of sheer agony, my legs lost their strength and I slid to the floor. The screaming inside my head had ceased and my inner demons had subsided back into my subconscious. I hoped Heather hadn't been caught up in the lesson that I'd just been taught. She'd already been through enough and she didn't deserve to suffer through further punishment.

I waited for the pounding in my head and for the dizziness to recede before I picked up the bracelet. It took another couple of minutes before I could force myself to stand. Tottering over to the dirt encrusted window, I examined my reflection. My eyes were wide and wounded. Forcing my mind to become calm wasn't easy, but my expression eventually smoothed out.

Something felt different inside me. Giving in to a hunch, I opened my coat and lifted my t-shirt up to inspect the hideous scar on my stomach. It wasn't as thick now and the black tendrils of evil had been reduced a little. The punishment that had caused me so much agony had also healed me slightly.

My lips twitched, then hysterical laughter spilled out of me. If Hagith and Orifiel had known that their torture would end up helping me, they would probably have used another method to cause me pain.

When I finally got myself back under control, I slipped the bracelet over my wrist. The spell became active again and Nathan appeared moments later. I put up a hand to stop him when he stepped towards me. "I'm fine," I said. The last thing I needed was for him to touch me. Neither of us seemed to be able to control ourselves when that happened.

"Who took you?" he asked. The abduction had happened so fast that he hadn't even seen who the culprits were.

"It was Hag and Orifice," I said with a sour mutter. I didn't care if they could somehow hear me. After what they'd just done, they'd lost any chance of ever gaining my respect, or my trust. I had a firm policy that torture wasn't the way to win people over to your cause.

His expression darkened. "What did they want?"

"They warned me not to 'sully' you again." I lifted my hands to make the obligatory quotation marks, then dropped them again.

"Did they hurt you?"

The pain had faded and I actually felt better, as if they'd recharged my batteries. "They didn't do anything that I couldn't handle." I waved away his concern without resorting to a lie.

It was obvious that he didn't believe me, but there was no point telling him what they'd done. It would only cause a deeper rift to form between them. We needed all the allies we could get, even if their methods were deeply questionable.

"I would very much like to know how they learned about what happened between us," he said.

Only after he voiced that concern did the same question occur to me. Our eyes met and we read the knowledge in each other's gazes. It had to be Brie. I was certain Sophia and Leo wouldn't have betrayed me like that.

The memory of the reading that Sophia had done for me came to mind, but I was pretty sure this wasn't the betrayal she'd warned me about. It was someone who was close to me that would stab me in the back. Brie and I were on the same team, but we were far from close. If she truly was responsible for tattling on me, there was zero chance that I'd ever call her my friend now.

"There's no point in saying anything to the others about this," I said. "Let's just take their warning to heart and try to keep our distance from each other from now on."

Nathan wasn't happy about it, but he nodded in agreement. "I am sure Briathos did not expect them to cause you pain." He was convinced that the teen was behind my punishment.

My mouth curved upwards in a mirthless smile. I'd be willing to bet she knew exactly what their plan had been. It was possible that she'd given them the idea to torture me. They were probably with her right now, recounting my screams of agony to her. Pain flared in my palms and I realized my hands were clenched tightly. I relaxed my grip and glanced down to see small bloody wounds in my flesh. Glad I kept my nails short, I gestured at the door. "We should get back to our patrol. You never know, we might actually have some luck and stumble across the next portal."

"We can only hope," he said with a strained smile. He touched me long enough to teleport us back to our original position, then pulled away again.

We walked side by side in silence, keeping some distance between us. Most of the snow from the storm had been cleared away from the streets now. Manhattan was once again a bustling hive of activity, yet the sidewalks were mostly deserted again. I hadn't seen it on the news, but the twelve bodies that had once been demons' vessels must have been found by the police. Our enemies made no effort to hide their slain rivals' hosts.

The few people who were out and about on foot scurried rather than walked. Their glances were furtive and afraid as they searched the faces of those brave enough to be outside. Unlike me, they couldn't see the evil that lurked inside the vessels that had been chosen to be the receptacles of evil.

My head turned constantly as I scanned for threats and searched for portals. There was no sign of the raven or demons as Nathan guided us away from the buildings towards a park. As we drew closer I saw we were at the very southern tip of the island. Water from the bay shimmered beneath the weak winter sunlight. As we entered the park, I saw a sign stating that we were entering the Battery.

Pigeons pecked at crumbs on the ground. The bird attack was still fresh in my mind and I eyed them mistrustfully. We skirted around them and walked along a narrow, winding path. Snow had been cleared from the walkway, but it still covered the grassy area. Trees were sparse and leafless, but squirrels were plentiful. They chased each other in an endless game and I envied them their sense of fun.

Spying us, a pair of squirrels raced over. They stopped a couple of feet away to beg for food. "Aw, they're so cute," I said. My heart melted at their hopeful brown eyes and bushy tails. "I wish I had some food to give them."

Nathan pushed something into my hand. I glanced down to see it was one of Sophia's cookies. "I am sure she will not mind," he said sheepishly. He wasn't supposed to use his power for trivial things, but he sometimes made an exception.

"How did you do that?"

"I can retrieve items if I know exactly where they are. I knew the cookies were in a jar in the kitchen and simply reached out with my essence and brought one to me."

"That is so cool," I said, more than a little jealous of his abilities. I hunkered down and broke off small pieces of the cookie. To my delight, the squirrels reached up with their tiny paws and took the food from me. Stuffing the bounty into their cheeks, they raced off back to their tree.

"You should do that more often," Nathan said wistfully.

"Do what?" I asked as I stood. "Feed the wildlife?"

"No. You have a beautiful smile. I wish I could see it more frequently."

I slid him a sidelong look to find him looking down at the ground. We were afraid to make eye contact, fearing what would happen if we lost focus again. "I haven't had a lot to smile about lately," I said quietly. "Seeing those little guys so happy brought me some joy, so thanks for that."

"You are welcome." I heard a lot more behind his few words. For the sake of us both, it was safer for them to remain unspoken.

Chapter Eighteen

I stopped every now and then to feed the squirrels as we made our way through the park. I hadn't had much chance to see the sights. It was nice to be able to just enjoy the city for once.

We kept our distance from the water. The entire island was warded by an invisible demon barrier. If we got too close, we could set it off and bring the hell spawn to investigate. I could see the Statue of Liberty far in the distance and knew I'd never get to see it up close. At least I couldn't while I remained trapped here.

Wandering past a circular stone building, I marveled at the aged architecture. The structure was in pretty good condition given its age. I glanced inside one of the square windows to see a cannon staring back through a metal grate. A sign said it was Castle

Clinton. A few tourists were walking around inside, staring at the sights. Apart from two small roundish buildings, there wasn't much to see inside. I wasn't tempted to investigate.

Following the path, we walked past a pier to another park. We didn't enter it this time and continued on until we reached the Hudson River. Turning north, we maintained a comfortable silence. There were many things that I wanted to say to Nathan that I couldn't. I was pretty sure he was suffering from the same problem.

Buildings lined the far side of the river. They were small compared to the skyscrapers in Manhattan. Our path curved and skirted alongside a museum with gray walls. Seeing a small stand of trees just ahead, I was surprised to see so much greenery. The trees still had their leaves attached. They appeared to be pines of some sort, so I guessed they were needles rather than leaves.

Two inhumanly handsome men were standing beneath the trees. From their expressions, they were having an intense conversation. Nudging Nathan in the side, I nodded towards them. "I think they're angels," I said at his enquiring glance. "Do you know them?"

He studied them and shook his head. "They do not look familiar." That didn't mean they weren't his kin. Anyone could be possessing the vessels. He wouldn't know who it was unless they introduced themselves.

They hadn't noticed us yet. Even if they did see us,

Nathan would just look like a normal human to them rather than a celestial being. The pair were now arguing and didn't notice it when thirteen figures appeared behind them. Scarlet light emanated from their hideous faces, giving away who and what they were.

Weapons appeared in the hands of two of the demons. Two others drew slender, clear bottles from beneath their robes. The rest descended on the unwitting angels and grasped hold of them.

Nathan took a step forward, but I caught his hand before he could go to their aid. He was badly outnumbered and something told me these weren't ordinary lesser demons. They were something far worse.

Instead of daggers or swords, their weapons of choice looked a lot like scalpels. Hands were clapped over the angels' mouths to muffle their screams of fear and outrage. Their clothes were torn open to expose their chests. Their screams turned to pleading, but were ignored. The demonic surgeons sliced through their flesh to reach their hearts. Then the two holding the bottles stepped forward. Bright white light spilled out of the opening and was drawn into the bottles.

The angels screamed in desolation and loss as their holy essence was stolen from them. They sagged to their knees when their vessels became empty of grace. Blood flowed from their deep, jagged wounds. They would die if they didn't receive medical attention immediately. Right on cue, their heads were tilted backwards and the scalpels were drawn across their throats.

Leaving the bodies to slump to the ground, the demons unceremoniously disappeared. Appalled that his kin had been destroyed right in front of him, Nathan left my side and appeared next to the bodies. He hunkered down beside them and put his hand on their foreheads. He shook his head in sorrow when he realized that he couldn't save them. What had been left of the angels had died along with their vessels. Their essence would live on, but the demons had trapped them in vials. We still had no idea why they were collecting them.

I raced over to offer Nathan some support and stumbled to a stop when I saw their faces. I'd thought they would revert back to their human guises when they died, but they were still inhumanly handsome.

Seeing the slices in their flesh up close, my hand went to the scar that marred my chest. It was the same type of wound that my mother had received that I hadn't even known about until after she'd died. For a long moment, I teetered on the edge of an epiphany. Then I fell over the edge into a realization that I could never come back from; my mother had once been an angel.

With the truth now evident, I couldn't believe that I hadn't seen it before. It was no wonder Sophia reminded me so much of my mom. They'd suffered exactly the same type of loss. Both had lost their grace and had been permanently trapped inside their human vessels.

Selfishly relieved that Nathan was lost in mourning, I turned away so he couldn't see my expression. Shock coursed through me and my mind was scrambling for an explanation. Questions wanted to spill out of me, but I kept them shut tightly inside.

My guardian had been there the night my mother had died and he hadn't saved her. I now wondered if he'd known her before she'd ceased to be an angel, but I couldn't bring myself to ask him. Did it even really matter? She'd had her grace taken from her and had been reduced to far less than the celestial being that she'd once been.

One question plagued me above all others. My mother had never told me who my father was. Now that I knew the truth about her origins, my old curiosity was aroused again. She must have met a man and had fallen in love with him and they'd conceived me. He'd either died, or had left her to fend for herself before I was born.

Sorrow for my mom almost overwhelmed me. She'd not only had to contend with losing her holy essence, she'd also been lumped with me. I felt ashamed of the grief that I'd caused her every time I'd been rebellious. She'd deserved better and I'd failed her.

Tears welled, but I refused to let them fall. I was filled with self-pity, yet my self-loathing outweighed it. What right did I have to feel sorry for myself? It finally hit me how selfish I'd been and how I'd always put myself first. I couldn't fathom why Fate had chosen someone as flawed as me to save humanity. How could I save the entire population of the world when I couldn't even save the one person who had meant everything to me?

Gathering myself, I turned to see Nathan laying the bodies to rest. He wore a look of sorrowful concentration as he put his palms on their lifeless chests. They began to sink into the ground and he sank down with them. They disappeared from view, then he returned alone. He held his hand out to me. I took it and laced my fingers with his. We were both filled with too much sadness to succumb to temptation this time.

He took us back to our base and I dropped his hand before Brie could unleash a scathing remark about me trying to suck his essence away again.

Sophia saw our expressions and was instantly concerned. "What has happened?"

Sam came thumping down the stairs, drawn by her alarmed tone. His hearing was just as good as an angel's. He burst into the room and took up a spot beside Leo. They didn't look anything alike, but their worry was nearly identical.

"We just witnessed Collectors harvesting two angels," Nathan said. His devastation was plain to see as he sank down onto his chair.

Sophia blanched and put her hand on her heart, just like I had when I'd seen the bodies. It was an involuntary reaction to hearing the news. She would have a scar just like my mother's. My feet were moving before I realized what I was going to do. I put my arms around her and hugged her tight. "I'm sorry," I said hoarsely. "I'm so sorry for what they did to you."

"Now you finally understand the danger that we face," Brie said to my back. I didn't need to see her expression to know it would be cold. "It is not just humans who will suffer if the demons break free from their cage. Our kind will be hunted down and harvested, just like the two poor souls that you saw being taken today."

I flinched at her accusing tone. It felt like she was blaming me for every theft of holy essence that had ever been stolen. "I'll find your grace," I vowed to Sophia. I didn't know how I would do it, or if it was even possible, but I meant it with everything I had. "I promise that I will find a way to fix you." Sophia stroked a hand down my hair, comforting me instead of the other way around. She didn't say anything, probably believing it was an empty promise. I leaned back and met her eyes. "I will," I said fiercely.

Her smile was sad. I knew she wanted to believe me, but she didn't dare to. If I were to fail, it would be yet another disappointment that she would have to suffer through. "I believe you will try," she said at last.

"Would you like some tea?" I asked. "I know I could use some." I also needed a few moments to be alone.

"I'd love some, thank you."

"Tea fixes everything," Nathan said so bleakly that Leo put a hand on his shoulder in comfort. That was something my mom used to say. It had never been less true than it was right at this moment.

Chapter Nineteen

By the time the kettle finished boiling, I'd settled myself down enough that the tray didn't rattle when I carried it to the table. Sam sat with his head bowed, watching the others from beneath his heavy brow. I could tell that he felt left out. He was an imp, the lowest of the low in hell. He had nothing in common with the three current, and one former angel, apart from a desire to lock the demons away forever.

Pouring Sophia some tea, I filled a cup for myself, then shifted my seat closer to Sam. He sent me a grateful look. The contact wasn't for just his benefit. He wasn't the only one who felt like an outsider. I didn't belong here either.

"What can you tell me about the Collectors?" I asked the room in general.

We all looked at Sam, hoping he'd have an insight

into the strange pack of demons. He gave a small shrug. "I have only heard of them through gossip." That was the lesser demons' favorite pastime, so it wasn't a surprise. "I have heard that they have been tasked with searching for angels, but I did not know that they were stealing their essence."

"They have to be keeping the grace somewhere," I said. "What I'd like to know is why they're taking it in the first place?"

"That is something we would all like to know the answer to," Nathan said. His face was drawn, yet he was still achingly handsome. I only allowed myself fleeting glances at him to prevent myself from becoming ensnared by his beauty.

"You don't have a book about them in your library?" I asked Sophia.

"I am afraid not. Most of the books were written by humans who were beneath the influence of angels. I do not have any books that were written by demons."

"You should not be wasting your time worrying about stolen grace," Brie said. Nathan flicked her a glance that bordered on being annoyed. It seemed I wasn't the only one who found her attitude to be abrasive. "Your task is to stop the gates of hell from being broken open."

"I know," I said crankily. "I don't need you to remind me about it every five minutes." I hated being told what to do. I hated it even more when the order came from a snotty little fourteen-year-old brat.

She raised an eyebrow in disbelief. "Are you certain of that? It would seem that you stray from your task far too often. Sometimes, it is necessary for you to be taught a lesson to put you back on the correct path." Her lips curved in a small, mocking smile.

Narrowing my eyes, I knew with utter certainty that she'd tipped Hag and Orifice off and had sent them after me. I bared my teeth in a tight grin that almost made her flinch. "Believe me," I said grimly. "I won't be forgetting the lessons anytime soon." I would never forget the torture that I'd received at the hands of the beings who were supposed to be holy and pure.

"Is there something going on that the rest of us do not know about?" Leo asked uneasily. Sam had slipped his hand into mine and was huddled against my side. Neither Brie, nor I answered, which was answer enough. "There should not be secrets between us," he said with a hint of anger. "How are we supposed to function as a group if we cannot be honest with each other?"

From the sly look in Brie's eyes, she was well aware of my secret. Hag and Orifice had obviously told her about Zach. She dangled the knowledge above my head, erroneously believing that it gave her power over me. I was about to shatter her illusion that I was the malleable child that she mistakenly believed me to be.

"I'm dating someone," I said. Profound satisfaction flowed through me when Brie's mouth dropped open in shock at my unexpected admission. "He was my boyfriend in Denver. He moved to New York and I ran into him a few weeks ago."

It was good to finally tell them the truth. I felt as if a weight had been lifted off my shoulders. It came crashing back down again when I saw the look of betrayal on Nathan's face. He looked away from me and his entire body was tense with pain.

Leo's mouth was open as well as he tried to articulate his confusion. "What? How?" Taking a breath, he organized his thoughts. "Perhaps you had better explain this in more detail."

Nathan crossed his arms and stared at the wall. He was unwilling to hear the story, but he made no move to leave. Brie's shock had turned to quiet glee at seeing everyone so put out by my news. Sophia fussed with her teacup, refusing to meet my eyes. Clearly, she wasn't happy about this either. I was pretty sure I knew what was bothering her.

"I can see what you're all thinking," I said, "and no, I am not sleeping with him." Nathan closed his eyes in relief and some of his tension seeped out. "We met by chance and we've had coffee together a few times."

"You are lucky the boy did not turn you in to the police. You did flee from the scene of your mother's death, after all," Brie pointed out.

"Zach knows I would never hurt my Mom," I said as evenly as possible. It was all I could do to resist the urge to throw myself at her and throttle her into unconsciousness.

"You knew about this?" Leo said to Sam, who was the only one who hadn't looked surprised by my bombshell. Brie's shock had been due to me admitting to the secret.

Shrinking down into his seat, Sam nodded timidly. "I have been helping Violet to sneak off and meet with him."

My guardian sucked in a breath and glared daggers at my best friend. "Don't blame Sam for this," I said sharply.

"Why did you renew your relationship with your beau?" Nathan asked. "Do you not realize how dangerous you are to him?"

I flinched at the implication that I would bring harm to my boyfriend. "His name is Zach Orion," I reminded him. I thought I'd broken him out of the habit of using such archaic speech. "I haven't told him anything about angels or demons. He has no idea about you guys, or that I'm supposed to save the world."

Brie was practically drenched in self-satisfaction now. "It would be selfish and stupid for you to continue seeing this boy. You should break it off with him immediately."

"Or what?" I said flatly. "You'll send Hagith and Orifiel to torture me again?"

Her face paled when Sam, Leo and Sophia looked at her with a mixture of accusation and horror. "I did not ask them to harm you," she defended herself. "I merely mentioned that I was concerned that your attention may have become divided."

In a quiet rage that I hadn't known he was capable of, Sam launched himself across the table. His hands wrapped around her throat as he knocked her out of her chair. "You. Do. Not. Treat. Friends. That. Way!" he said, banging her head against the carpet to emphasize each word.

Leo dragged him off while his twin glared at the imp in hatred. "Violet is not my friend," Brie spat. "She is a soulless vessel that is quickly filling with evil. Soon, she will burst and infect us all!"

My face twisted in disgust at the image her description brought to mind. I pictured my body as a balloon that grew bigger and bigger until it popped, spraying my putrefying guts everywhere. "Eww, gross," I said in complaint, then shocked her when I sniggered.

"How can you laugh at a time like this?" she said in outrage and scrambled to her feet. Any injury that she'd sustained from Sam's attack had already healed.

"Because I'm not an emotionless robot like you," I said. "I'm human and we tend to laugh, cry, scream and yell whenever we feel strong emotions." My tone was as patronizing and condescending as I could possibly make it. After her declaration that I was basically a walking bag full of pus, I felt no desire to hide how I felt about her.

"I cannot believe you tattled on Violet," Leo said. The look he gave his sister was full of disappointment. He turned his back on her and looked at me. "Did they hurt you?"

"She said they tortured her," Sam reminded him. "Of course she was hurt!"

"It wasn't that bad," I replied, but they didn't believe me. "I mean, it didn't tickle, but I'm fine. No lasting damage was done." None that I knew of anyway.

"The only lasting harm that has been done was the injury the Wraith Warrior gave you," Brie pointed out. "Thanks to your stupidity at being drawn into yet another demon trap, it was able to pinpoint your location."

"I guess that means I am stupid as well, since I was with Violet both times when she has become trapped," Leo said flatly. Every time Brie opened her mouth, she dug herself into a deeper hole.

"This bickering is getting us nowhere," Nathan said in a harsh tone. "Briathos is correct, Violet needs to break up with the boy immediately."

I could almost feel the jealousy coming off him in waves. "That's not going to happen," I replied. Even when my guardian was the one giving the orders, I still didn't like it.

"Why do you insist on seeing him?" Sophia asked. She was barely able to hide her exasperation with me.

Sam came to my rescue before I had to try to explain my reasons for not wanting to let Zach go. "She did not ask to be chosen to save the world." His words were quietly dignified and even Brie appeared to be listening to him. "She went from being a normal teenager, to an orphan who is expected to fight the denizens of hell. Zach is the only normalcy she has in her life right now. Surely, she deserves to find some happiness among the horrors that she will have to go through?"

Nathan's face fell at the thought of me finding happiness with someone else. "Does this boy mean so much to you then?" he asked me.

I realized I was twisting my ring around and around and stopped. I gulped down my fear and nodded. "I care about him and he cares about me."

Angels might not be able to cry, but their vessels could. I saw tears shimmering in his eyes. Then he nodded in acknowledgement of my words and disappeared.

"Fabulous," Brie said snarkily. "Now you have driven one of your allies away."

"It's a pity it wasn't you," I said just as spitefully. "Feel free to join him anytime."

"I would be delighted to," she responded and zapped herself away as well.

Slumping back in my chair, I put my hands over my face in despair. I'd never wanted to hurt Nathan and I'd just torn his heart out. He knew there could never be anything between us, yet he couldn't stand the thought of me being with someone else. We were in a no-win situation where everyone would end up being hurt.

Chapter Twenty

Nathan and Brie still hadn't returned by the time I went to bed, which filled me with trepidation. I wasn't concerned about Brie, of course. She could disappear forever for all I cared. I was worried that Nathan was so disgusted with me that he was never coming back.

Lying on my side facing the wall, a tear slipped out before I could stop it. I held back a sob at the thought that I'd lost my guardian forever. We might not be able to love each other like I fantasized about, but I couldn't stand the idea of him not being in my life.

"Do not cry," the object of my thoughts said from behind me. I tried to roll over to face Nathan, but he put a hand on my shoulder to stop me. "I have given the matter some thought and I have come to the conclusion that this is for the best."

"What are you talking about?" I couldn't hide the

tremble in my voice. I was terrified that he had decided to leave me.

His answer was a surprise. "That you continue to date Zach." His tone was anything but happy despite his decision. "Samuel was correct. You deserve to find some happiness in this harsh existence that you have been thrust into. If the boy brings you joy, then you should be allowed to spend time with him." He took a breath and his hand tightened on my shoulder momentarily. "I only have one request."

I would have given him the moon if he'd asked for it. "Name it."

"I would ask that you do not consummate your relationship with him yet."

I heard the pain in his voice as I tried to figure out what he meant. Then it dawned on me. "Are you asking me not to have sex with Zach?"

His hand tightened again and I felt him shudder. "Yes," it came out sounding strained. "I know it is a lot to ask. You are human and you have wants and needs that angels cannot truly understand." They could if they let their vessels take back some of their control. Unfortunately, when that happened, the consequences were grim. "I would just request that you postpone the consummation until after we have accomplished the task that Fate has given you."

"What happens then?" I didn't want him to voice the answer, but he did anyway.

"Then you will no longer need me and I will leave you in peace forever."

I was glad I was facing away from him. I didn't want him to see my devastation at the prospect of us never seeing each other again. "I promise I won't sleep with Zach," I said as my tears began to fall. He stroked his hand down my arm in thanks, then disappeared from my room. "I love you, Nathan," I whispered to the empty room, then turned my face into my pillow so it could muffle my sobs.

Sometime during the night, my sobs petered out and I fell asleep. I found myself in the shadowlands of my mind. Standing in small clusters, the legion turned when they sensed my arrival.

At my curt gesture, Morax and the other Demon Lords crossed to join me. I made sure we were far enough away from the lesser demons and captains so they couldn't hear us.

"What do you require from us?" Morax asked. They still looked spooked from the rain of holy fire that had swept through them, but they were intact. My advisor was far more cooperative than usual. He didn't ask me what had happened. I guessed they'd already figured it out for themselves.

"What do you know about the Collectors?"

Exchanging uneasy looks, they knew I wouldn't be satisfied with anything less than the truth. "They are tasked with hunting down angels and extracting their holy essence," he replied.

That much I'd already known, but at least I knew Morax wasn't lying. "Where do they take the vials that are filled with grace?"

"You have witnessed a harvest?" he asked in surprise.

"Yeah. Thirteen demons appeared and carved open a couple of angels. I saw them extract their grace. I need to know where they take it."

"Why?"

"I want to find Sophia's grace and give it back to her."

Morax stared at me for a long moment with a blank face. "I do not know where the grace is taken." I couldn't be absolutely sure, but I had a feeling he was telling me the truth again.

"What are they doing with it?"

He shrugged his massive shoulders. "I am not privy to that information."

"Why do I even bother to ask you guys anything?" I said in disgust. "You never have any answers for me."

"Our new master is so secretive that we do not even know who he is," one of the other lords informed me. "He sends his orders to us using various minions. He is not the type to divulge his plans to us. It is not our fault that we do not have the answers you seek."

Her logical reasoning just infuriated me all the more. "You suck," I said and she blinked in astonishment. "You all suck," I added petulantly. I knew I was being childish, but I was unable to stop myself from venting.

"Do you feel better now?" Morax asked mockingly.

"Would you perhaps like to cry on my shoulder?"

My response was grumpy. "I'd need to climb a ladder to reach your shoulder." The thought of attempting to console myself with my demon advisor almost made me grin.

"Perhaps you should ask the scribe," the female lord suggested and hiked her thumb over her shoulder towards the house. "He has spent more time in a palace than any of us. He may have the answers that you seek."

"Thanks," I said and willed myself over to the house. I was learning different tricks each time I entered the shadowlands of my mind. It seemed that I had my own form of teleportation here. I wished I could use it when I was on Earth. The only time I'd managed to shift myself was when Brie had almost stabbed me in the stomach. My inner demons had teleported me to safety then, but they hadn't repeated the action since.

At my knock, the curtain on the door was pulled aside. Heather's face lit up and she opened the door. "Hi," she said and pulled me into a hug. "I didn't expect to see you again so soon."

"Me neither," I admitted. I had no control over when I ended up in this place. Dire need could sometimes bring me here, which seemed to be the case this time. "Were you hurt when the angels punished me?"

She paled slightly and shuddered. "No, thank God. We could hear the demons screaming and the entire house lit up with this blinding white light. Sy and I didn't feel a thing, though. The house shielded us from whatever it was that they did to you." The rest of my mental hitchhikers hadn't been so lucky.

"That's a relief. I was worried you might have been caught up in it, too." I looked around and couldn't see her companion. "Is Sy here?"

She pointed at the living room, but I didn't see him sitting on the couch. "He's in there," she said and led the way into the room.

Moving closer to the couch, I saw him sitting on the floor. He was hunched over a sketchpad, carefully drawing a rune. His forked tongue was poking out slightly in fierce concentration.

"What are you up to, Sy?" I asked.

His head jerked up in surprise and alarm. He relaxed when he saw it was just me. "I am working on creating a new rune."

"What does it do?" I was fascinated at his ability to come up with new spells.

"I do not know yet," he confessed. "I will probably never get to find out." He was forlorn that the symbols he worked so hard to create might never be used.

"Can't you try them out to see what effect they'll have?"

He shook his head dismally. "I do not have blood in my veins when I am in my spirit form." He was practically just a ghost now, as were all of the residents that were squatting in my head. Runes required blood and flesh to be able to be activated. The legion might look solid, but it was just an illusion.

"What if I use my blood?"

Hope filled his scarlet eyes at my proposal. "You would be willing to test it?"

"Sure. What harm can it do? But I have a question first." At his enquiring look, I elaborated. "Do you know why the Collectors gather angel grace and what they're doing with it?"

He shook his head. "I do not know much. The Collectors are former scribes," he explained. "They were chosen by the Hellmaster and were given the task of finding holy essence. I do not know where they take the grace, or what their plans for them are. That knowledge is reserved for those in a far loftier position than the one I held. I was basically just an apprentice. The Head Scribe would most likely be able to answer your questions."

He watched my face anxiously and I was pretty sure he was telling me the truth. I'd seen him attempt to be untruthful before. For a demon, he was a terrible liar. "Who is he and where can I find him?"

"His name is Dantanian." He scowled as he said the name. It was obvious that he didn't like his boss. "He resides in the Scriptorium in the capital city in the first realm."

"What is a Scriptorium?" I pictured an ancient building with columns and dusty bookshelves.

"It is the building where the records of all runes that have ever been created are kept."

"If this demon is in the first realm, then I won't be able to ask him about the stolen grace," I said dourly. I hadn't even been to the seventh realm yet. It would be weeks or possibly even months before I'd find the entrance to the innermost realm. That was if the toxin that was spreading inside me didn't kill me first.

"May I choose a rune to test now?" he asked.

"Yeah. Go ahead." I waved at him to commence his experiment and he flipped through his sketchpad. Settling on one of the symbols, he looked around, searching for a place where he could paint it. Most of the walls were covered in paintings that I'd conjured up. None of the walls were blank. With a thought, I cleared a wall for him to use as a canvas. Then I made a paintbrush appear in Sy's hand.

We walked over to the wall and I called my dagger into being. It sliced into my palm and blood welled. Sy dipped his brush into the cut and I willed the pain away so I didn't feel it when the bristles entered the wound. Heather made a face, but hovered behind me to watch as the rune came to life on the wall. He dabbed the brush on the symbol a few more times, then stepped back. "There. It is complete." He sounded both proud and satisfied.

"Let's see what it does," I said and placed my palm in the center of the rune to activate it.

Bright scarlet light flared and a circle about a foot wide opened on the wall. It was so deep and dark that I couldn't see where it ended. From Sy's startled expression, he hadn't expected a pit of nothingness like this.

"It's just a hole," Heather said, sounding profoundly disappointed. "Does it do anything?"

Sy was about to answer, but he didn't get a chance to speak. Wind sprang to life so suddenly that we reeled backwards from the blast. It began to spin in a circle and instead of pushing me away, I felt it tugging at my clothes as it tried to draw me towards it.

The wind picked up and the sketchpads that Sy had worked so hard to fill with runes were sucked up off the floor. His pencils joined the sketchpads and spun around and around in a dizzying circle. Books flew off the bookcase to the left of the strange hole. The pages fluttered madly and some were torn out completely.

Increasing in intensity, the vortex was inexorably drawing the furniture towards it now. Heather let out an alarmed screech when her feet left the ground. Our hair was tossed around and our clothes flapped loudly. Sy was smart enough to dive behind me to use me as a shield.

Willing myself to be anchored to the ground, I grabbed hold of Heather before she could be swept into the mixture. I watched with my mouth gaping open as a pencil disappeared into the hole.

"No!" Sy shouted in anguish when his sketchpads flew towards the magical opening next.

Finally regaining the ability to think, I pushed Heather and Sy away where they'd be out of danger. Then I leaped forward and scraped my dagger over the edge of the rune. Only a thin sliver of the symbol showed, but it was enough to nullify the spell. The wind immediately died, but a second pencil became lodged in the wall. If the scribe had made the rune any larger, the consequences could have been catastrophic.

Heather's hair was a mess and her eyes were wide with fright at how close she'd come to being sucked into the hole. It was too small for her to fit through, but she might have been hurt. "Maybe you'd better not practice that one again," she suggested shakily.

"Did you see it?" Sy crowed in delight. His fear had been replaced with pride at his accomplishment. "I wish the other scribes had been here to witness that."

"Congratulations," I said and clapped him on the back. "You just created a mini black hole." I had no idea where the pencil that had been sucked into the hole had disappeared to. It was probably in another recess of my mind.

"It is just as well that I did not create that rune while I was still in the clutches of the Head Scribe," Sy confessed. "If the Hellmaster and Princes had this sort of power at their hands, they would wreak havoc on Earth."

Demons constantly vied for power and were never content with what they had. They rose through the ranks as high as they could go and dreamed of deposing their masters so they could take their place. One of them had somehow overthrown Satan, hence the reason why he was no longer in charge. Where he'd gone to was a mystery to everyone except the being who had defeated him. I was pretty sure it was one of the princes, but no one in the legion could confirm it. Their new boss was an enigma to them as well.

Chapter Twenty-One

Brie had returned to our base sometime during the night. I entered the front room and froze in mid-yawn when I saw her sitting at the table. "Oh. You're back," I said with as much distaste as I could muster. I was beyond the ability to pretend to like her now.

Sophia nudged me out of the way with a disapproving frown. She carried my breakfast on a tray. The heavenly scent of waffles drew me in her wake. "If we are all going to continue to live and work together, then I insist on everyone acting in a civil manner," she said.

"I don't think 'civil' is in Brie's vocabulary," I replied as I plonked down on my seat. Sam and Leo exchanged a quick smile that dropped away when Sophia glared at them.

"I am surprised you even know the word

'vocabulary'," Brie retorted just as nastily.

Nathan held up a hand to silence us. His expression was eerily serene. He could control his emotions far better than I was able to. "Sophia is right. It is time to put our animosities behind us. We are all working towards the same goal. We are here to support Violet in her cause."

"Which cause is that?" Brie said sulkily. "Getting into her boyfriend's pants?"

"Ouch," Leo said with a wince. "That was catty even for you."

"You're really becoming one with your vessel," I said in mock admiration. "You sound exactly like a bratty little girl."

Horrified by my accusation, Brie turned a stricken look on Sophia. "Can that be true? Have I been in this vessel for so long that I am already becoming more human?" She said it as if it was the worst thing that could possibly happen. To her, it probably was.

"No," Sophia said and flicked a brief glance at Nathan. "It takes centuries for that to happen."

"Unless my evil influence is speeding up the process," I mentioned nonchalantly. "All that rot inside me could be spreading out to infect you guys as well." I gave an inward chuckle when Brie inched her chair away from mine. Only Nathan and I knew there was supposedly a cure for my affliction. It seemed he hadn't mentioned it to them yet. Until we discovered how to rid myself of the poison, there wasn't much point in getting their hopes up.

"You are not evil," Sam declared. "I would sense it if you were."

Pulling my plate closer, I cut my waffle into sections. Sophia had smothered it in syrup, the way I liked it best. "Can't you feel the evil that the Wraith Warrior's injected into me?" I asked.

He shook his head. "Not anymore. I could when it first happened, though. Perhaps your legion is healing you?" It came out sounding hopeful.

"Maybe," I replied, then stuffed some waffle into my mouth. I knew the torture that Hag and Orifice had doled out to me had diminished the toxin. I also suspected that the effect wouldn't last long. Once it wore off, the rot would begin to spread again.

I'd almost finished my breakfast when Leo spoke. His usual cheery smile was gone and he was uncharacteristically serious. "Nathan and Sophia are right. We need to stop squabbling and focus on our task. We have to find the next portal."

"It isn't like we aren't trying to find it," I said with a sigh. "Apart from searching the city during our patrols, I don't know what else we can do."

"Speaking of patrols," Brie said. "It is my turn to escort you today."

My response was swift and emphatic. "Hell no!"

"You do not trust me," she said flatly.

"Is that a joke?" I searched her face and didn't see a smile anywhere. "You tattled on me like a five-year-old and your buddies zapped me with holy fire. So no, I absolutely in no way shape or form trust you. I will *never* trust you now."

Pushing away from the table, I abandoned what was left of my breakfast and stomped towards the door. I grabbed my boots, but I didn't bother with my coat. I was careful not to slam the door behind me as I escaped into the cool air outside. Sophia didn't deserve to have a broken door just because I was in a bad mood.

Leo joined me a few seconds later. I had one boot on and was hopping on one foot trying to get the second one on without falling over. "Do you realize how ridiculous you look?" he asked.

Finally managing to don the boot, I snatched my coat out of his arms. "Don't start on me."

He realized I was close to tears and wisely said nothing as I stalked off down the street. Even as upset as I was, I still searched for enemies both in the sky and on the ground as I struggled to get into my coat. "Your sister is unbelievable," I said when we'd walked for a few blocks.

"Brie is not technically my sister," he replied then subsided at my glare.

I hated being corrected almost as much as I despised being told what to do. "Why does she even stick around if she hates me so much?"

"For the same reason that none of us will abandon you. You are our only hope against the forces of evil."

His tone was far too reasonable and it grated on my nerves. My teeth ground together in an effort not to take out my anger and frustration on him. Unlike

Brie, I actually counted Leo as a friend.

Eventually, I calmed down enough to walk at a normal pace rather than stomping along like I was trying to punish the concrete. My feet carried me to my favorite area of the city. We meandered along Fifth Ave and I managed to get some window shopping in while searching for threats.

My eyes passed over the window of a café then I did a double take when I saw Zach. He sat next to a girl with honey colored hair, big brown eyes and an impressive chest. Her tight red dress was obviously expensive. It revealed a cleavage that drew the stares of any male within sight. She wasn't as inhumanly beautiful as an angel, but she was still gorgeous. She put her hand on Zach's arm and leaned in to say something. He laughed at whatever she said and my blood boiled in instantaneous jealousy.

"Um, Violet, are you perhaps feeling a strong emotion right now?" Leo asked in a strained voice.

"You could say that," I said, striving for control. "Why do you ask?"

"Because your eyes are glowing crimson."

Aghast to hear that, I whirled around to stare at my reflection in the window. He was right, my eyes were glowing, but only faintly. Shock robbed me of my fury and the glow faded until they were back to normal.

When I turned around again, Zach and the mystery girl were leaving the café. He chivalrously helped her into a long black coat with fur trim. She buttoned it up, then leaned in and pressed her breasts against his chest as she tried to kiss him. He turned his head at the last second so her lips landed on his cheek rather than on his mouth. She gave him a disappointed pout before climbing into a waiting town car. The window drew down and she waved coyly before the driver sped off.

"Let me guess," Leo said slyly. "That is your beau?"

"Not you, too," I groaned. "His name is Zach."

"Who was the girl who just tried to kiss him?"

"I think her name is Candice Weller. Zach's Dad and her Mom are trying to set them up." From the look of it, both families came from money. Their combined wealth would probably be enough to buy half the buildings in the city. Or maybe all of them. Taking stock of my life, I realized I had absolutely nothing to offer my boyfriend. I was a penniless waif who was living on the charity of an ex-angel.

Staring after the town car broodingly, Zach took his cell phone out and typed something. I took my cell phone out just in case and my heart leaped into my throat when I saw a message from him. His text said that he missed me and he wanted to meet me tomorrow afternoon at three-thirty.

"I take it you have received good news?" Leo said dryly when my face lit up in a smile.

"Its excellent news. He wants to meet me tomorrow." I texted back that I was on board with the idea. He responded immediately, naming our favorite café as a meeting place. It was several blocks away from here in a less expensive area.

Zach received my message and his brooding expression was replaced with a happy smile. He touched the necklace that I'd given him, then sauntered off towards his home. In my jealous rage, I hadn't even noticed that he was wearing it. A few seconds later, a man left the protection of a doorway down the street and trailed after him.

"Who is that?" Leo asked.

"That's Giles. He's a bodyguard who doubles as a chauffeur."

"Exactly how rich is your boyfriend?"

"Very," I said dryly. "If you take us to Park Avenue, I'll show you where he lives."

His curiosity was too great to resist my offer, so he zapped us both there. We were half a block away from the twenty story building and I pointed at it. "Zach and his Dad live in the penthouse."

Leo's head went back and he stared up at the fancy balconies far above us in awe. "What does it look like inside?"

"It's gorgeous. There's black and gold marble everywhere and they have a grand piano. Zach has an entire wing to himself and even has his own kitchen and chef." Leo slanted a look at me and I knew what he was thinking. "I have no idea what he sees in me," I said. "Now that I've seen Candice, I'm even more confused. She's beautiful, rich and comes from the same world that he does."

"You are prettier than she is," he said staunchly,

but he couldn't argue with the other points that I'd made. I didn't fit into Zach's circle and I never would. In his own way, he was just as unsuited to me as Nathan was. Or to be more accurate, I was unsuitable for them.

Chapter Twenty-Two

Leo whisked us back to the café and we resumed our patrol. I mulled over my options as we walked. A few minutes later, he nudged my side and pointed at a pack of demons across the street. We didn't try to follow them this time. Neither of us wanted to be drawn into another trap and suffer more embarrassment. We merely watched them from a distance until they entered a building.

"Nice try," I scoffed when they disappeared from our sight. "We're not going to fall for that one again."

It was doubtful that the hell spawn had known we were there. There were probably groups like this wandering around their chosen turf all over the city. They were trying to lure us into their lairs. They were using the same trick on us that we'd used on them. If it hadn't been for the raven's intervention, we wouldn't have stumbled into the last trap at all. Thanks to the bird, I was now tainted and had a death sentence hanging over my head.

After an hour of randomly walking around, we headed back towards Midtown. "I have a confession to make," I said when we were halfway back to our base.

Leo braced himself for the information that I was about to lay on him. "What is it?"

"I didn't get this ring from a cheap jewelry store."

He blinked in surprise and glanced at the ring I was wearing on my left hand. "Where did you get if from?"

"Zach bought it for me. It's a real ruby and the band is platinum."

Taking my hand, he brought the ring up to his face to take a better look at it. "This must have cost him a fortune."

"I know." I still couldn't believe he'd spent so much on me. "That's one of the reasons why I don't want to break up with him."

"Because he buys you expensive baubles?" he said with a frown of disapproval and dropped my hand.

"No," I laughed. "It's because he's so thoughtful. He might be a spoiled rich kid, but he's a really nice guy despite his upbringing."

"Is that even possible?" he joked, which made me laugh again. That was one of the things I loved about the teen. He could always make me smile no matter how depressed I was feeling.

When we drew closer to our lair, we took pains to make sure we hadn't been followed. Leo took no chances and teleported us inside when we were still a few blocks away. Nathan, Brie and Sophia were huddled at the table. To my surprise, Sam was sitting with them rather than watching TV. He was glaring at Brie with his arms crossed. She ignored him as if he didn't exist. Their conversation broke off when they realized that we'd returned.

"I want you to bring Hag and Orifice here," I said to Brie without preamble.

"Violet," Sophia said in the exact same tone that any parent would use as a warning. My mom had never bothered to scold me. Her response whenever I was being a pain was to give me a sad look. That was always enough to cut me to the bone and to make me feel remorseful.

Heaving a sigh, I tried again. "It would be great if you could ask Hagith and Orifiel to join us for a meeting." My tone was exaggeratedly polite, but Sophia nodded her approval anyway.

"Why?" Brie asked suspiciously.

"Because we need to clear the air. Like it or not, we're supposed to be allies. Maybe it's time we started acting like it."

She looked at Leo, Nathan and Sophia for their opinions. When they all nodded, she reluctantly agreed. "Fine. I will return shortly."

"What are you up to?" Nathan asked as soon as she was gone.

"Nothing," I replied and headed to the kitchen. He was on my heels before I'd made it through the door.

"I know you," he said in a low voice. I wasn't sure he even realized how seductive he sounded. I shivered and closed my eyes for a second. "I can tell when you are planning something."

"How can you know me that well?" I said over my shoulder as I filled the kettle. "I thought you only popped into my life whenever I was in danger of dying." He remained silent for so long that I turned to face him. My eyes widened at his guilty expression. "How often did you watch over me?" I asked softly so the others couldn't hear me.

His gaze flicked to the door to make sure we weren't being observed. "Far more often than I should have," he replied just as quietly. "I watched you from afar during the day and I watched you while you slept at night. I have been with you almost every moment of your life since I rescued you from that toy chest when you were two. The only time I have not been with you was the night your mother's life was stolen."

That last part gave me a stab of pain, but my mind went straight to another conclusion. My face flamed and I took a step back. I should have felt violated at discovering his constant presence, but my mind was filled with visions of him watching me as I soaped myself in the shower.

He chuckled and moved closer. He lightly brushed his thumb over my flaming cheek. "I said almost every moment, Violet. I would never violate your privacy as I am sure you are imagining that I have right now." I closed my eyes and pressed my face against his palm. He let his touch linger for a moment before pulling away.

"I really don't have a devious plan in mind," I said as I set the kettle on the stovetop. "I just think we need to join forces with these douchebags." He winced at my choice of terminology. "I'm sick of them hiding in the shadows and watching me like I'm some sort of criminal. They could be doing something far more constructive than that."

"Such as?" a familiar voice asked snottily.

My back went stiff when I realized it was Hag and that she'd overheard me. I glanced over my shoulder to see her and her sidekick, Orifice, standing in the doorway. "I'll let you know just as soon as I've finished making tea," I said evenly. I didn't want them to know how fast my heart was racing at seeing them again. My inner demons reacted to my instinctive fear and quivered inside me. They could only hear and see what I could when I was under a lot of stress. I imagined they were getting a clear visual of the angels right now.

"We will join you shortly," Nathan said and motioned for them to head over to the table. They obeyed him with reluctance.

Thankfully, it took several minutes for the kettle to boil. I was able to calm my fears, but I didn't object when Nathan poured the water into the teapot and picked up the tray. He knew how badly my hands were shaking. Apparently, he knew everything about me. My face went red again at the knowledge that my guardian had watched over me so diligently and I'd never even known he was there. The only time I'd been able to see him was when he'd saved my life.

"You look flushed," Sam said when I took my seat. Hagith and Orifiel had chosen to remain standing, which was good because there weren't enough seats for us all. "Is your illness returning?"

"I don't think so," I replied.

"What illness is this?" Hagith asked in a sharp tone.

"Violet was attacked by a Wraith Warrior," Sophia informed them as she poured tea for us both.

"I'm surprised Brie didn't tell you that when she ran to you to tattle on me," I said.

The teen sent me a sullen look. "I did not think it was important." She'd told them that Nathan had used his grace to heal me, but she hadn't bothered to tell them why it had been necessary.

"Of course it is important," Orifiel said in shock. "How is she still alive?"

"Because I'm Hellscourge," I said before anyone could offer their opinion on the subject. "I think you keep forgetting that." This was what I'd been mulling over while Leo and I had been out on patrol. "I was chosen by Fate for a reason." I met their stares and saw only contempt and disgust in Hagith's and Orifiel's eyes. They really hadn't liked being called douchebags, even if it was an accurate assessment of their personalities.

"There has never been anything like me before," I continued. "Or so Fate told me. I'm the only one who has ever defeated the master gate to hell. You guys can't even enter the shadowlands." Now it was my turn to show them contempt. "Even with all of your holy power, you're pretty useless in this war."

Hagith sucked in an affronted breath and Orifiel puffed out his chest. I plowed on before they could utter their protests. "Nathan made a point earlier that I think needs to be repeated for everyone's benefit." By everyone, I meant them. "*I'm* going to be the warrior in this war. You guys are just the lackeys. So, the next time you believe I've stepped out of line and you feel the need to dominate and torture me, remember this; without me, you won't have any way to defeat the minions of hell. If I'm not on your side, you will lose this war."

Nathan masked his smile, but Leo didn't bother to and grinned widely. Sam was staring at me adoringly. Even Sophia looked almost proud. Brie was the only one who looked like she'd just finished sucking on a lemon. Her sour expression was priceless.

"What are you saying, exactly?" Hagith demanded.

I pushed my chair back and stood. Placing my hands on the table, I leaned forward to stare them directly in the eye. "I'm saying that I want you both to back the hell off. Stop threatening me and my boyfriend. I'll date him if I want to and no one in this room can stop me." Nathan closed his eyes in pain, but I swallowed my guilt down. This wasn't really about Zach. It was about establishing boundaries. "You don't own me. You aren't my boss. You don't get to tell me what to do. I'll do whatever it is that Fate has planned for me, but I'll do it on my own terms."

"What if we do not agree to your terms?" Hagith said. Fury filled her to bursting, but Orifiel had his hand on her arm to control her. His thoughtful frown indicated that he was taking me seriously.

"Then you won't be my allies anymore. You'll just be an obstacle stopping me from doing what I'm meant to do because you're so hell bent on trying to control me."

"It has already been proven beyond a shadow of a doubt that giving free will to mankind was a grave error," she stated. Breaths of shock were sucked in.

"Hagith!" her sidekick said in a shocked whisper. "Be careful what you say!" He cut a look at Nathan, who had hunched his shoulders slightly.

Straightening her spine even more, she stared down her nose at me. "I only speak the truth and you all know it."

"I don't disagree with you," I said, to her shock. "Humans have made all kinds of mistakes and they never seem to learn from them. I'm just telling you that I'm not going to be your puppet. I'll listen to your advice, but I'm not going to let you control me."

They exchanged a look, then turned to Brie. She was staring at me speculatively, weighing their options. She knew me well enough by now to know that I'd been pushed to my limits. If they shoved me over the edge, the consequences would be unpredictable. Not even I knew what would happen if they went too far. Being tortured had been the last straw. I wasn't going to let them have that kind of power over me ever again.

"It seems that we have no choice," Brie grated. "We cannot take away your freedom to make your own choices. I just pray that they will be wise rather than foolish ones that will end in the doom of mankind."

From her posture and expression, she was already convinced that any choices I would make would be poor ones.

Chapter Twenty-Three

With our agreement hammered out, we settled down to discuss strategy. Two more chairs were produced from somewhere and Hagith and Orifiel reluctantly sat down at the table.

"What sort of progress have you made in locating the next entrance to hell?" Hagith asked, deliberately looking away from me. She directed the question at Nathan.

"We have spent nearly every day searching for it without success," my guardian replied.

"Randomly searching the streets is obviously not working," she said with a critical sniff.

Orifiel took over when he sensed our unified dislike that our efforts had been dismissed so easily. "Perhaps a more structured plan would be in order," he suggested.

Sophia shook her head. "You cannot plan when Violet will discover the portals. Like the visions that I am sent, she will only find it when it is the right time." Either Leo had shared my theory with her, or she'd come to the same conclusion on her own.

Neither of the new additions to our group looked happy about that. They wanted to take control and become my puppet masters even after I'd told them I wouldn't cooperate with them. Clearly, it was in their natures to tell others what to do.

"How do you intend to proceed then?" Hag asked. She flicked a glance at me and I took it as an invitation to speak.

"We'll just keep bumbling along, stumbling across the portals either by accident, or wait for Sophia to be sent a vision. It's worked for us so far and I have no reason to believe that it will stop working. Fate wants us to win. She isn't going to let us down."

My answer didn't appease her. "I am not comfortable relying on an entity such as Fate to guide you through such an important task. It should lie in the hands of beings who are more qualified to make critical decisions."

She was talking about her and her trusty sidekick, of course. "You don't have any choice here," I said without sympathy. "Fate set me on this path and she's kept me alive so far. I trust her to make sure I can stop the coming apocalypse." I trusted Fate far more than these two. All they'd shown me so far was their sense of superiority and willingness to torture me to make me behave. At least Fate had warned me that I'd suffer during this journey. She hadn't ambushed me and tortured me with holy fire.

"Orifiel and I will join your group in your patrols then," Hag decided. "The more of us that are out searching, the quicker we will locate the next portal."

I rolled my eyes inwardly when it became obvious that she hadn't listened to a word we'd said. She just didn't get that she had no control here. They could search the streets all they wanted, but it was highly doubtful that they would be able to spot one of the entryways to the otherworld. I was the only one who seemed to be able to see the doorways.

"Agreed," Brie said before anyone on our team could offer a protest. She sent me a warning look not to ruin our tentative alliance with her friends. It was clear that she had chosen a side and that I wasn't on it.

"There is no point in delaying any further," Hag said and stood. "Orifiel and I will report back if we find anything of interest." Her sidekick stood and the pair disappeared.

I was glad that they hadn't stuck around. Their constant mistrustful glares in my direction had grated on my nerves. The moment they were gone, Sam stood and headed upstairs.

Leo watched the imp leave in amusement. "I am surprised he managed to tear himself away from his beloved programs for this long."

"Me, too," I replied with a small grin.

Brie sniffed and crossed her arms. "His addiction to television is unhealthy. The device should be removed before he becomes completely useless to our cause."

"Is that the way you treat all of your allies?" I said in disgust. "Take away everything that makes them happy so they can be as miserable as you are?"

"I am not miserable," she denied. "I am perfectly happy."

Her mouth was set in a grim line that was anything but happy. "You're locked out of heaven and you're stuck in a teenager's body," I reminded her. "You are clearly not glad to be in this situation."

"The only thing that I despair about is being stuck with a creature that is as vile as you," she shot back. "Even the imp has more purity than you do. At least he still has some form of his soul, as twisted as it is. You do not even possess a soul at all."

Nathan shot her a look that brimmed with anger. Leo's face was full of disappointment. Sophia saw how much the barb had hurt me and compassion filled her. Out of all of them, she was the only one who understood what it felt like to be soulless. Losing her essence wasn't quite the same, but it came close.

"I'll try to spare you from my vileness in the future," I said stiffly and stood.

"She did not mean that how it sounded," Leo said in a futile effort to pardon his sister's behavior.

"Yes she did," I refuted. "She meant exactly what she said."

Brie didn't argue and I felt her smug look on my back as I left the room. I headed upstairs to the living room. Sam glanced up and froze when he saw my face. "What happened?" He'd obviously been too engrossed in his show to listen in to our conversation below.

"Brie was just being her usual charming self," I replied and sank down into the armchair.

His expression darkened, but he wasn't surprised. "Sometimes, I think we would be better off without her," he said quietly in an effort not to be overheard.

"I wish we could vote her off the team, but we need her." He didn't look convinced. "Her spells have come in pretty handy so far," I reminded him.

"I suppose," he said with a reluctant nod. "I just wish she did not despise us both so much."

A small part of me was glad that I wasn't the only one on her hate list. Sam had only ever been helpful, but she couldn't get past the fact that he was an imp. In her eyes, he would never gain redemption for the things that he'd done in the past.

I opted to read rather than watch TV, but I had trouble focusing on the words. Worry was eating at me. The longer I waited to retrieve the next piece of the object and to kill the Demon Prince, the worse my health would become. I hated the thought of the poison spreading through me, but I didn't know what the cure was yet. I had a feeling my health was going to get much worse before I would find a solution to this problem.

Chapter Twenty-Four

After my training session the next morning, I watched Sam attempt to defend himself from Leo. The teen was patient with the imp. It was fun to watch them working together. They should have been enemies, but instead had become friends. It was a miracle that everyone except Brie had so readily accepted Sam into our circle.

I was pretty sure his gradual transformation was helping with that. While he'd been as ugly as sin when he'd first joined us, he wasn't as hideous now. His brow wasn't as pronounced and his eyes were less squinty. His skin had changed from pitch black to an unhealthy dark gray. He wasn't as thin now, either. His ribs and spine weren't quite so prominent.

Being back on Earth was slowly restoring him to his human form. Helping us seemed to be making up for the bad karma that he'd gained during his stint as a pirate. His sins would have sent him to hell eventually, but the pirate captain had dragged him there bodily when Sam had defied him. The pirate was also a captain in hell's armies. He had been the first demon to become trapped inside me. He hadn't been alone for long and he had a lot of company now.

Nathan popped in and out during the day. He was avoiding my eyes, which told me he was still hurting that I was dating someone else. I almost wished I hadn't run into Zach by chance and renewed our relationship. But a small, selfish part of me was glad I had a chance of normalcy with someone.

Speaking of Zach, I opted to take Sam with me when I went to meet my boyfriend later that afternoon. Frankly, I didn't trust any of the others not to try to scare him away.

"You're getting better at fighting," I said as we made our way towards the café.

Sam made a rueful face and rubbed a spot on his side where he'd been stabbed with the blunt end of the stick. He healed far faster than I did and the bruise had already faded. "If you say so," he said in a doubtful tone.

"You didn't see how bad I was when I first started."

He smirked slightly. "Leo told me that you tripped over your own feet and almost impaled yourself on his weapon. I wish that I had been there to see it, it would have been very funny."

I sniggered at the memory of how inept I'd been. "I'm almost grateful to the legion for giving me their fighting abilities."

"It is good that they are finally useful for more than merely causing pain and torment," he agreed.

In a strange turnabout, the demons that had taken up residence inside me were more helpful than our new angelic allies. None of them had caused me earth shattering agony like torturing me with holy fire. Or maybe *unholy* fire would be more appropriate in their case.

We reached the coffee shop where I'd arranged to meet with Zach a few minutes before three-thirty. Sam dropped back to blend in with the wall. As always, he would stand watch from across the street. I'd arrived early so Giles the stalker wouldn't see me sneaking inside. I went in and ordered, then found a table in the corner away from the windows. Sam wouldn't be able to see me now, but he would find a way to warn me if danger approached.

Several minutes later, Zach stepped inside. He was right on time, as always. He scanned the room and didn't immediately see me in the sea of faces. I waved my hand at him and he instantly smiled and made his way through the crowd. He was wearing his school uniform and had a black leather satchel slung over his shoulder.

"I've missed you," he said as he took his seat and plonked the satchel on the floor between his feet. He reached for my hand and we twined our fingers together.

"Have you?" I was still pissed at the memory of seeing Candice Weller pressing her breasts against him.

"Of course." He gave me an easy smile, then frowned when he studied my face. "Are you feeling okay? You look a little pale."

"I'm fine." I felt okay at the moment, but I was pretty sure that wouldn't last for long. Once the rot began to spread inside me again, I was bound to go downhill pretty fast.

"After what happened to me yesterday, I was worried that my love of coffee shops would be spoiled forever," he said mournfully. "Now that I'm here with you, I'm enjoying the experience again."

"What do you mean?" I decided to play along rather than confront him with what I'd seen. He didn't seem particularly happy about his coffee date with my rival.

His expression darkened slightly and he scowled. "Do you remember that dinner my Dad wanted me to go to? The one with Clarice Weller and her daughter?"

"You mean Candice?"

He nodded. "Yeah. Her." His tone dripped with distaste. A surge of gladness swept through me to hear it. "Well, my Dad and Clarice obviously thought we'd hit it off," he continued. "They decided to set up a date between Candice and me. We had coffee together yesterday."

Their parents sounded almost as manipulative as Hag and Orifice. "Why didn't you just say no?"

He looked at me in disbelief. "I sometimes forget that you haven't met my father. He's not exactly the kind of man you can say no to."

"So, what happened during your date? Did it go well?"

He huffed out a sigh. "If you call listening to her babble on and on about herself a date, then it went great. I barely said a word, yet she somehow took that to mean I'm interested in her." She'd probably thought he was too enraptured by her beauty to be able to form words. Most of the guys who had been staring at her had seemed to be fairly dumbstruck.

"Can't you just tell her you're not into her?"

He hesitated, then shook his head. "It isn't as simple as that."

"Why not? It seems pretty clear to me. She wants you, you don't want her. Just say so and she'll leave you alone."

This time, his expression was almost pitying. He obviously thought I was being naïve. "You know my father is a banker." It was a statement rather than a question, but I nodded anyway. "Clarice Weller has a lot of money tied up in his bank. He needs me to play along with Candice until they've cemented some kind of deal."

I stared at him in disbelief for a moment. "Are you saying that your father is pimping you out?"

He laughed loudly enough to draw attention from some of the nearby patrons. His grin melted away and realization set in. "Actually, now that you've mentioned it, that does seem to be what he's doing."

I didn't want to ask, but I had to know the answer. "Does this mean we're over?" I said in a small voice.

He was alarmed and tightened his grip on my hand. "No! I'll never break up with you. I told you that you're the only girl for me and I meant it. We were made for each other."

I stared into his eyes and became mesmerized. We weren't even kissing and the heat was already rising in me. "What are you going to do? Date both of us at the same time? I'm not really the sharing type, you know."

The thought of him kissing someone else made my blood boil. *He's mine, not hers.* At that thought, I took a mental step back. The legion was taking my lust a step further and it was now becoming possession. I loved Nathan with all of my heart, but I felt something for Zach, too. I just wasn't sure what it was yet.

"I'll pretend to date her if I have to," he said, "but I promise I won't kiss her. I'll tell her I'm still getting over a previous relationship and that I want to take things slowly." That was what I'd asked him to do and he'd complied with my wishes so far. I was fine with kissing him, but I wasn't ready to get naked with him yet. Especially after the promise that I'd made to Nathan.

"Good," I said in satisfaction. Candice might be

dating him in public, but I was the one who he really cared about. We leaned in for a kiss and the heat instantly became scorching. I grabbed hold of his coat and drew him in closer. Our mouths melded and we became lost in passion.

I had no idea how much time had passed when a sudden loud noise forced us apart. Someone across the room had spilled their drink all over another patron and an argument had broken out. I picked up my tea to find it was nearly cold. I felt self-conscious that we'd been kissing in public for so long. Amused looks were sent our way and I sank down in my chair in embarrassment.

"That was intense," Zach said. His hair was mussed and I didn't even remember running my hands through it. I checked mine to find it was still in neat braids. I was very glad we were in a coffee shop rather than his bedroom. God only knew how far we would have gone if we'd been alone. I wasn't even sure the promise I'd made would have stopped me from tearing Zach's clothes off. My lust for him was starting to get out of control.

Chapter Twenty-Five

Zach checked his watch and couldn't hide his disappointment. "I have to go. I managed to ditch Giles in a nearby library. I'd better get back there before he realizes I've snuck out."

"What would a rich kid like you need to go to the library for?" I asked in amusement.

"I'm studying Latin and ancient Greek. The books are too rare and valuable to be taken out of the library. I go there to do my assignments." That explained why he'd been carrying the satchel.

He wasn't just a pretty face. He was also smart. I felt even more insignificant now that I knew he was learning ancient languages. "That's a pretty handy excuse," I admitted.

"Giles usually drops me off, then sneaks in to spy on me," he explained. "He stays for a few minutes to make sure I'm really doing my homework, then he usually leaves. I guess libraries are too boring for him to stick around for very long." He checked his watch again, then picked up his satchel and stood. "He'll be coming to pick me up soon."

I stood as well. I gave Zach a final kiss, then waited for him to leave the café first. I watched through the window, but no one seemed to be following him. His ruse had worked and he'd managed to sneak away to see me without his stalker knowing about it.

Pulling the door open, I stepped out. Sam appeared at my side after I'd taken a few steps and shook his head at me.

"What?" I said defensively.

"Sometimes, I forget that you are a teenager as well as being the scourge of hell. Your hormones must be difficult to control at your age."

Technically, he was over four hundred years old, but his mortal age was the same as mine. He didn't seem to be suffering from the same affliction that I had. He was still too much of an imp to even think about dating. "You saw us, huh?" I said in embarrassment.

"Yes," he confirmed. "I had a strong feeling that I should check on you. I managed to sneak into the coffee shop and saw you with your boyfriend. You were too distracted to notice that everyone was watching you both. Some were even filming you with their cell phones. I had to trip someone and get them to spill their coffee on someone else to gain your attention."

I groaned in fresh humiliation. Zach's back had been to everyone, so hopefully his identity would remain unknown. I was still wanted by the police and having my face appear on the internet was the worst thing that could happen right now. "The others will kill me if they find out about this," I muttered. Sophia owned a computer, but she rarely used it. With luck, the police wouldn't be able to identify me if they came across the videos. Sam was the only one who was addicted to watching TV. I could only cross my fingers and hope our two new allies didn't stumble across the footage if it appeared anywhere. "We should head back to the store," I said. Someone would come looking for us if we delayed for much longer.

We saw three groups of demons on our way back to our base. Neither of us were tempted to follow them without backup. It was obvious that they were trying to lure us into a trap. For creatures pretending to be human, they were terrible actors. Their expressions were far too nonchalant to be believable and they moved stiffly.

Making note of the buildings that they disappeared into, we continued on our way. Since neither of us could teleport, we took great care to make sure the raven hadn't followed us. We even took a circuitous route just in case hidden eyes were watching. When we were two blocks away from our base, Sam drew me in close to the nearest building. He used his talent to camouflage us as we made our way back to the store.

"How did your date go?" Brie asked me with heavy sarcasm when we stepped into the room.

I froze for a moment, horrified that they might have somehow seen the videos of me kissing Zach. Nathan looked slightly annoyed rather than devastated, and I realized she was just being her usual bratty self.

"It went fine," I replied. I wasn't about to tell them that Zach was being forced to see another girl by his own father. As if my life wasn't already complicated enough, another spanner had been thrown into the works. Zach might not like Candice now, but spending time together would give her the opportunity to work on him. She was beautiful and rich, just like him. She had far more in common with him than I ever would.

"Would you like some tea?" Sophia asked. I opened my mouth to answer, but nothing came out when I realized she was now staring straight through me. The distant look on her face was a sure sign that she was having a vision.

Sam and I hurried over to the table to take our seats. We'd just settled into them when she snapped out of her trance. It had only lasted for a few seconds this time.

"I take it you just received a vision?" Nathan asked. He was studiously not looking at me. Even though he'd agreed that it was for the best for me to date

Zach, it was still painful for him.

"Yes," Sophia confirmed.

"What did you see?" Leo asked.

"I was shown a cathedral somewhere in the city. The portal must be somewhere nearby. Demons cannot step onto consecrated ground." She directed that last comment at me and I filed the information away.

Brie frowned slightly. "There are many cathedrals in Manhattan. Can you tell us anything that might help narrow our search down?"

"I only caught a fleeting glance of the building. It was enough to see that it was surrounded by fences that are topped with razor wire. It appeared to be in disuse."

"I think I know which cathedral it might be," Leo said. "If it is the one I'm thinking of, it is in Morningside Heights."

"Do we have any bottled demon blood handy?" I asked and Sophia nodded. "Great. We'll wait for dark, then Leo can zap us there."

Nightfall was only half an hour or so away now. I had enough time to scoff down a meal, then it was time to go. Sophia packed a backpack with a container of blood and some paintbrushes. Food and water wouldn't be necessary. My bodily functions became nonexistent when I was in the underworld. That was something I was very grateful for. Trying to find a restroom in hell was pretty much impossible.

Before we left, I ducked upstairs long enough to

grab my favorite black jacket, then returned to the others. We gathered into a group and Leo teleported us elsewhere. We appeared on a sidewalk next to a low stone wall topped with wrought iron. It was too dark to make out what was beyond the fence, but it seemed like a large open area. A green sign with white writing told me it was Morningside Park.

Swiveling around, I saw that Leo had deposited us directly across from the cathedral. Sophia looked up at the building and nodded. "This is the place that I saw in my vision."

It was a cloudy night and I didn't have the benefit of the legion's night vision while I was on Earth. A single lamppost weakly illuminated a small area out front of the edifice. I squinted up at the structure, but couldn't make out much.

A car crested the hill to our right and its headlights washed over the church. Instead of the elegant structure that I was expecting, I saw a weirdly shaped building that seemed to have been designed by several different architects. It was a strange mishmash that made little sense.

Four smaller sections jutted out at the front of the building. Three of them were roughly circular, but the fourth was rectangular. Little about them was uniform. Even the windows on each section were different. I could see the main part of the building rising high above the smaller ones. They were clustered around it like frightened children seeking solace from a stern parent.

The stone was dark and grimy and was in dire need of a good scrubbing. A trio of robed statues frowned down at us from the rectangular section of the cathedral. I caught a glimpse of more statues high above us. Then the car turned into a side street, plunging the building into darkness again.

I'd noticed one more thing before the light had faded. Just as Sophia had seen in her vision, a fence had been erected around the church. It was topped with razor wire that would shred me to pieces if I tried to scale it. The church had been built on a tier above us. Below it was a stone fence that acted as a boundary.

"We should walk around the perimeter and see if you can locate the portal," Nathan suggested. If demons couldn't step onto consecrated ground, then that meant the entryway to the shadowlands had to be somewhere outside the property.

Opting to walk downhill rather than uphill, we followed the stone fence. It wasn't in the best of repair and was falling apart in some places. We passed a stretch that had been defaced by graffiti that looked like it had been drawn by a child. It appeared to have been there for several months. No one had bothered to clean it off yet. I doubted that anything would be done about it anytime soon.

We reached a small section of the wall that had been fenced off with chain link. It was meant to keep the stones from falling onto unwary pedestrians. Deep shadows caught my eye and I turned my head to see a dark doorway carved into the rock. The others walked right past the optical illusion that the fence was whole. They didn't see the gloomy passageway that led to the shadowlands.

"The portal is here, guys," I said before they could get too far away.

They trudged back and stared at the fence blankly. "Where?" Leo asked.

I put my hand on the stone. The wards that had been erected around the city also blocked the portals. Only one had been left open for the demons to enter and exit from hell. I had to unlock the ones I discovered with a rune that Sytry had shown me. "I can see a portal behind this wall," I told them.

Sam was carrying the backpack that had been bought as a replacement for the old one. Our previous one had been mauled by a hellhound. We'd had no choice but to abandon it in the palace of the eighth realm. He slipped it off and rummaged around inside, taking out the container of blood. He handed it to me and I cracked the lid open. The blood smelled rank, yet also sweet. It was cold and had congealed from being refrigerated. He handed me a paintbrush next and I went to work. It only took a couple of minutes to construct the symbol. Since there wasn't a door that needed to be unlocked from both sides this time, I only needed to paint the rune once.

Leo took the brush from me when I was done. He flicked it and the blood disappeared.

"That's a neat trick," I said with a grin. "I wish I could do that."

He shrugged and shot a guilty look at Brie's frown. It was beneath them to use their celestial powers for such mundane tasks. "It is just a small thing," he said modestly.

Nicking my palm with my dagger, I pressed it against the rune and crimson light flared. The blood dried instantly as the symbol became activated. I pushed my hand through the shimmering illusion. To them, my hand and half of my arm disappeared.

"I wish we had some idea of where the next piece of the object is located," Nathan said. He was trying to hide his worry, but it came through loud and clear.

"I have a plan," I said as confidently as I could manage.

Leo smirked. "I cannot wait to hear this."

"We're going to break into the palace and torture the Prince until he tells us where he's hiding it."

Brie rolled her eyes. "That is a stupid plan. You are almost certain to fail."

"Do you have a better idea, Princess?" I said with heavy sarcasm. "No? Well then, shut the hell up until you think of something useful to say." She quivered in outraged indignation, then disappeared.

Sophia let out a small sound of disappointment, making me feel guilty. "I do wish you two would at least try to get along."

"Sorry," I said and almost meant it. "Brie just really rubs me up the wrong way."

"I am certain she feels the same way about you," the clairvoyant said and gave me a hug. "Good luck, Violet. Try not to get caught." To Sam's surprise and embarrassed delight, she gave him a hug as well.

Leo pulled me in and smacked a kiss on my cheek, then grinned at Sam. "Do you want a kiss, too?"

"That will not be necessary," Sam said with quiet dignity.

"I guess I will just have to give you a hug instead."

They gave each other a brief embrace, then Sam turned to Nathan. They weren't as close and didn't feel the need to embrace each other. "I will guard Violet with my life," Sam vowed.

Nathan nodded and offered the imp his hand. They shook solemnly, then my guardian turned to me. We knew better than to get too close to each other. We stood a few feet apart as he searched for something to say. "Stay safe," he said at last. I could sense that he wanted to take me into his arms, but we both knew that it wasn't a good idea.

"I will. We'll be back before you know it." I blew him a kiss, then took hold of Sam to guide him through the portal.

Chapter Twenty-Six

Damp stone walls flanked us as we made our way along the cobbled path. The walls were covered in sickly looking yellow lichen. My skin crawled at the thought of touching it. The walls rose so high into the air that it was impossible to tell if it was ceiling, or sky above us.

Mist swirled around our ankles, creeping higher with each step. It was knee deep by the time we drew closer to the end of the alley. I couldn't pinpoint the exact moment that we stepped out into the shadowlands. The walls were suddenly gone and the ground had changed from cobbled stone to hard-packed dirt.

"I really hate this place," Sam whispered. He huddled close to my side and peered around at the mist.

"I'm not a big fan of it either." Anything could be hiding in the fog, stalking us and waiting for our backs to be turned so it could leap out and chew our heads off.

Stop being so melodramatic, Morax scoffed inside my head. *You are getting spooked for no reason.*

There's plenty of reason, I argued. *Remember the trials we had to go through to defeat the master gate? Any of those creatures that it threw at us could show up at any time.*

That is unlikely, he disagreed. *It is almost unheard of to discover a gate that leads directly to Earth from hell. The hellgates have no reason to keep this area guarded by anything dangerous.*

His calm reason reassured me and some of my tension seeped away. It was almost comforting to have the legion inside my head. They would come to my aid whenever I was in danger. It wasn't because they cared about me, but for their own self-preservation. If I died, so would they, or so we all assumed.

My watch had stopped working the moment we left Earth, but I judged that an hour or so had passed before we finally saw the giant black wall that enclosed each realm of hell.

The flapping of wings alerted us that we weren't alone. I instinctively ducked just as the raven that had been plaguing me swept through the place where my head had just been. It must have been watching us when we'd been searching for the portal. It had waited for me to unlock it before following us inside.

Sam fumbled for the steak knife that he'd brought with him and I reached for my dagger. It began to glow and something stirred in the fog. Cawing loudly, the skeletal bird's noise drew it towards us.

So much for your theory that there's nothing dangerous lurking around here, I thought to Morax sourly.

If you believe that these foes are dangerous, then Fate should have chosen someone else to be Hellscourge, he shot back. Then we had no more time for arguing. One of the creatures launched itself at me and I understood his scorn. It might be freakishly large, but it was just a rat. My dagger slashed out to decapitate the rodent. Made of shadow, it was just an illusion and faded almost before it hit the ground.

Hacking and stabbing, we walked backwards towards the wall with the pack swarming all around us. Their teeth and claws were sharp enough to cut through our clothing and to reach our flesh. Cursing beneath my breath, I kicked at the closet rat. It was the size of a pit bull, but was far more vicious. It went sailing off into the gloom with an enraged squeal.

My back hit the wall, leaving me with no escape route. Standing beside me, Sam's eyes frantically searched the shadows as he panted in fear. By themselves, the rats weren't particularly fearsome. Dozens of them were approaching us, which meant that we were in trouble. Morax was poised to take over the fighting if it became necessary, but I had a better idea. "Gate!" I shouted. "Show yourself!"

The slick black rock at my back shivered and

turned to metal as the hellgate obeyed my summons. I glanced upwards to see a face forming. Eyes looked down at me, then rolled in a very human gesture. "Oh. It is you. I might have known."

His voice was identical to the master gate's, but his personality seemed gloomier this time. Twin gargoyles, made of the same black stone as the walls, roosted on the top of the gate far above us. The raven was perched between them. It glowered down at me with its single milky eye.

"Did you create these rats?" I asked. The illusions had all been created by the gates. They roamed around the shadowlands, waiting to be called into battle during the nine trials. Since I'd defeated the master gate, I didn't need to go through the trials again.

"They belong to me," he confirmed as the rodents slunk closer. Their beady black eyes watched us, searching for openings that they could exploit.

"Would you mind calling them off?" I asked with exaggerated patience.

Heaving a sigh, his mouth turned down in an unhappy frown. "Must I? It has been so long since I have had any entertainment. Seeing a pitifully weak human battle my creations would break the endless monotony."

"Get rid of them!" I ordered as they swarmed towards us.

He waited until the last possible moment before banishing the rats. Sam cringed beside me, shielding his face. He took a cautious peek, then dropped his hands when he saw that they were gone.

I turned to glare up at the gate and caught him smiling cruelly. "Thanks for acting so quickly," I said sarcastically.

His expression turned innocent and he lifted a brow made of wrought iron. "What? You were not harmed."

"How many times have you been defeated?" I asked. Getting out of hell wasn't as easy as simply finding a gate and conquering it. Princes and lords were the only ones who had defeated a gate in all nine realms. Some of the stronger captains could leave hell, but only if they'd conquered at least five gates, including one in the ninth realm.

All demons had to leave the underworld through the ninth realm. So far, very few of them had found a shortcut to Earth from any of the other realms. I was pretty sure my ability to find them was because I'd defeated the master gate. Doing so had given me privileges that no one else had. Sam and I should have been the only beings that this gate had ever seen, but I had the distinct impression that this wasn't the case.

"I have never been defeated at this particular location," he replied.

That made me blink. "Wait a minute. You can change location?"

"Of course," he said, as if it should have been obvious. "There are many areas where demons can challenge us from. We simply shift ourselves to wherever we are required to appear. You are the first being to ever enter this realm from a portal that comes from Earth." That gelled with the theory that I'd just developed.

"I take it you're guarding the entrance to the seventh realm?"

"I am," he said dismally. Even his gargoyle sentries were despondent. They glared down at us gloomily. The raven was gone. I assumed it was winging its way to report that I was about to invade hell again to its master. The gargoyles might be restricted from tattling on me, but the Hellmaster had his own eyes and ears to spy on me.

"Would you mind opening to let us through?" I didn't know why I was being so polite, it seemed mean to make him feel even worse than he apparently already did.

"I suppose I should," he said at last. "That is my purpose, after all. I was designed to act as a portal and nothing more."

Made of wrought iron just like the other gates, I noticed a difference in his design. Instead of being covered in decorations of humans being tortured in every possible way, they appeared to be reading, writing or playing music. "Do you enjoy the arts?" I asked as a crack appeared down the middle of his face.

"I do," he confirmed with a heavy sigh. "But it is my fate to never be able to read poetry, or to hear a harp play. Instead, I guard this dismal realm, penning in its occupants and keeping out anyone who does not have the right to pass."

Feeling bad for him, I trudged through with Sam at my side. The gate barely waited for us to get clear before it wheezed shut with barely a squeak of rusty hinges. His morose face faded and disappeared and the gargoyles went still again.

I waited until we were well out of earshot before I spoke. "Was it just me, or was that gate suffering from deep depression?"

"It was not just you," Sam confirmed. "I actually felt sorry for it."

"Me, too." We shared a look then I shook my head. "We must be getting soft." Allowing ourselves to feel sorry for anything in this place would be a mistake.

Chapter Twenty-Seven

This was the third realm that we'd been to so far. Each one was caught in a state of perpetual twilight. There was no real day and night, or sun or moon for that matter. It was always dim and dismal here. With each area that we entered, it became warmer and the air smelled worse.

As always, the ground was dry and parched. The soil was a dingy gray and the few trees we could see scattered around the horizon were black. They'd petrified long ago. Dark patches at the base of the trees were hell's equivalent of ponds. Snakelike things lived in the smelly sludge and they were always hungry. They could sense vibrations in the ground, so getting too close could prove to be dangerous to the unwary.

From what my inner demons had told me, the

outer realms were smaller than the inner ones. We'd been able to see the palace that lay in the center of the ninth realm from the master gate. It had taken us longer to reach the palace in the eighth realm. I assumed it would take us even longer this time. Luckily, we didn't have to walk all the way there.

At that thought, twin pairs of glowing crimson eyes appeared a short distance away. The nightmares were made of shadow and pulled a carriage that had once belonged to a Demon Lord. We'd appropriated it and now it bore my face on the door.

When the carriage pulled up alongside us, I was dismayed to see that my picture had changed. My skin was darker and the horns were more pronounced. My eyes were faintly glowing crimson.

Seeing the changes compelled me to check on the wound that I'd received from the Wraith Warrior. I lifted my shirt and jacket to that see the scar on my stomach had worsened. It was thicker and the tendrils had grown slightly. They were slowly writhing, almost as if they were alive.

"I do not like the look of that," Sam said in a disturbed tone. "Are you in any pain?"

I shook my head and let my clothes fall back into place. "I don't feel any different yet." He opened the carriage door for me like he was my lackey and we climbed inside. The plush seats were covered in black leather and thick black carpet lay on the floor. "We should avoid as many villages as we can and head straight to the palace," I decided. I didn't want to be here any longer than was absolutely necessary.

Telepathic, the nightmares read my thoughts and took off. They went from a trot to a dead gallop in mere seconds. Their hooves made no sound, but the wheels clattered over the hard ground.

Thick black curtains covered the windows. We glanced out every now and then to see small villages in the distance. It wasn't always possible to avoid them. As we drew closer to the city, they became more and more numerous. Each town held the souls of humans who had sinned enough to be sent here after death. Even above the racket of the wheels, I could sometimes hear their moans and cries of pain as we swept past them. I wasn't tempted to peer outside to witness their torture.

Eventually, I caught sight of the red beacon that acted as a landmark. It was only a faint spot on the horizon to start with. Each time I stuck my head out the window to check on our progress, it became clearer. Perched high atop the palace, it was the only way I could be sure that the nightmares were carrying us in the correct direction. Neither of them liked me very much. It wouldn't surprise me if they took us out into the wasteland and left us stranded there.

Sam had his head out the window to check how close we were getting. He pulled back inside to give me an update. "I can see the palace," he said. At a rough estimate, it had taken us nearly two full days to reach the outskirts of the city that was the capital of the seventh realm.

I pushed my window up to take a look and saw the city ahead. The palace sat on the top of a hill that was shrouded in gloom. A wall surrounded the city. It, and the buildings, were made of the same black rock that all of the structures in hell were made of. The beacon blazed brightly. It was impossible to miss when we were this close.

"We should stop short of the city," Sam advised. "If the demons see your image on the door, they will realize who is inside. It would be wise for us to avoid drawing attention to ourselves."

He was right, of course. Having my face on display for everyone to see would make it hard for us to sneak in. The nightmares were already slowing down without me needing to shout the order. Reading my mind, they headed away from the gates to the wall that curved around the city.

We pulled up about half a mile away and climbed out. "Thanks, guys," I said to the hellhorses. They snorted derisively and disappeared, taking the carriage with them. "That's what I love about hell," I said to Sam dryly. "Everyone is so friendly here." He sniggered nervously and we hurried towards the wall.

Somewhere in the distance, I could hear moans of desolation and cries of pain. I couldn't see the human souls that were being tortured, but they were somewhere in the vicinity.

We reached the wall without being spotted and examined the slick rock. The fence was only ten feet high. It acted as a boundary rather than a deterrent.

No one in their right mind would attack a city full of demons, which said a lot about me when I thought about it. Then again, I wasn't going to attack the populace. I was just here to take down the prince and to find the object that he was guarding.

"I will give you a boost," Sam offered. Buildings had been erected only yards away on the other side of the wall. They would give us cover as we infiltrated the city. He cupped his hands together and lifted me high enough to pull myself up. I leaned down, grabbed his hand and pulled him up beside me. Now that I was back in hell, I could call on the legion's strength and speed again. I was no longer a puny mortal, but had become Hellscourge, a figure of dread and legend come to life.

In this world, I was able to take on the worst demons and conquer them. Even Hag and Orifice should fear me when I was in this dimension. Luckily for them, they weren't able to enter the underworld. No angel could ever enter this domain without suffering terrible pain.

Chapter Twenty-Eight

As each realm grew bigger, so did the population and the cities that surrounded the palaces. Demons didn't need to sleep, so the streets were never empty. It wasn't going to be easy to avoid being spotted with so many minions bustling about as they performed their menial tasks.

Starting at the base of the hill, we worked our way up through the winding, random pathways. Sam held my hand and walked with his other hand touching the buildings. Whenever anyone came along, we pressed our backs to the wall and blended in with the stone. Without him, I never would have survived through the ninth realm, let alone have made it this far.

We kept to the narrower streets rather than taking the main road that carriages used. We could hear them rumbling uphill on the cobbled stones in a steady procession. "The Prince must have called a meeting," I whispered to Sam. Demon Lords and captains were travelling to the palace with their entourages in tow. The place would be crawling with enemies by the time we reached the top of the hill.

"Do you think they know we are here?" he whispered.

I shrugged. "Maybe. I haven't seen the raven since we left the shadowlands. It acts as the eyes and ears of the Hellmaster. It could have sent a warning to the Prince."

"Is the new master of hell not aware that the Princes are trying to kill you?"

I'd been thinking about that and had an answer ready. "I think he's counting on it because he knows that I can kill them. If he really was one of them as we suspect, then I'm killing off his possible rivals."

"Then why did he try to blast us with lightning when you killed the Prince of the eighth realm?"

"I'm pretty sure it was just for show. He was pretending to be outraged so his minions don't revolt when they realize how little he cares about whether they live or die."

"You are probably right," he said. "Demons do not have any compassion, or the ability to care about anyone except themselves. It would have taken treachery and betrayal for him to have risen so high. If it was possible for him to usurp the true master of the nine realms, then perhaps one of his rivals might be able to topple him off the throne."

I was still determined to take down all of the princes despite the fact that I would be doing my enemy's dirty work for him. Murdering their leaders threw the realms into chaos, which could only aid our cause. It was my hope that, even if the gates of hell were busted open, the troops would be in too much disarray to overrun our world.

We climbed up through the tiers until we reached the base of the palace. It was surrounded by a thirty-foot-high wall that neither of us could easily scale. It took us over an hour to walk around the perimeter, searching for a way in that was less populated. The only entrance we found was the main road that carriages were still streaming through.

Ending up back where we'd started, we peered up the wide path to see a large yard surrounding the palace. Guards were stationed every twenty feet or so along the driveway that led to the front entrance. There was nothing to offer us any cover. We weren't going to be able to sneak past them without being seen.

Carriages were lined up in front of the palace. Gray undead nags pulled the ones that belonged to captains. Nightmares pulled the others that belonged to the lords. The nags shifted uneasily at being in close proximity to their shadowy cousins. Nightmares tended to look at other animals as food.

Lords, captains and their entourages of five lackeys each were disembarking from their carriages. They hurried inside the front entrance where a group of guards were keeping watch. Their minions followed them inside.

This palace was three stories high. A tower speared upwards from the center of the building and stretched far into the sky. The scarlet beacon at the top of the tower cast red light on the grounds. We couldn't see it from this angle, but the prince's chamber would be on a separate tower that could only be reached by a short walkway.

"We will have to enter the yard and follow the wall to see if there is another entrance that is less well guarded," Sam whispered.

We slunk into the grounds, making sure to keep in contact with the wall so he could keep us camouflaged. Moving slowly was necessary for us to remain undetected. Although we blended in with the rock seamlessly, the illusion didn't work quite as well when we were in motion.

The prince had planned well when he'd had the lesser demons build this place. He'd ensured that no one could approach his domain without being seen. It wasn't just demon sentries that were stationed on all four sides of the palace. Gargoyles were perched on each corner of the roof on all three levels.

They weren't the same as the stone monsters that were part of the hellgates. These were made of flesh and bone. Squat and ugly, they were black and their faces were vaguely ape-like. Leathery wings wrapped around them, hiding their bodies. Tails with arrow shaped tips were coiled around their clawed feet.

They watched the grounds diligently.

"The whole place is being guarded," I whispered to Sam when we'd performed a full circuit of the property. There were four entrances and all were being watched by soldiers and gargoyles. "How are we going to get inside?"

I felt rather than saw his shrug since we were both camouflaged against the wall. He thought about it, then came up with a solution. "We could attempt to slither along the ground."

"I guess we can give it a try," I said with great reluctance. The front entrance was the widest and the guards were clustered off to one side. We would have the best chance of entering through this door without bumping into someone.

My instincts warned me that this was a bad idea, but I couldn't think of a better one. We sank down to our knees, then lay down on our stomachs. It wasn't easy to coordinate our movements when we had to hold hands the entire time. I made a face at the thought of how encrusted with filth my clothes would be by the time we reached the building.

That concern didn't last long. We'd only travelled a few yards before I lost contact with Sam. Without his camouflage, I instantly became exposed. A gargoyle swept its eyes across me and went rigid. It stared down at me with its head cocked to the side, trying to figure out what I was. Sam reached for my hand and the creature opened its mouth. We disappeared and blended in with the ground, but it was too late to hide. It gave a high-pitched shriek that alerted guards and gargoyles alike.

"Try to stay still," Sam said. "Maybe they will not be able to find us."

I moved my head just enough to look up at the palace. The gargoyle that had spotted me dived off the rooftop. Its wings spread out to reveal a hairy body that was vaguely humanoid. It zoomed towards me with its feet outstretched. I ducked my head and bit back a scream when its claws tore furrows down the entire length of my back.

More gargoyles followed after it, all aiming for us. They couldn't see me, but they could see my blood that had just splattered on the ground. Guards were running in our direction, confused about what was going on.

Sam realized our cover had been blown and yanked me to my feet. Shouts rang out when we were spotted. We sped back down the road just as a final carriage was entering. We split up and sprinted around either side of it. The Demon Lord looked out the window just as I ran past. The painting on the door was an exact replica of his face. Both wore identical scowls. He roared for his nightmares to stop, inadvertently blocking the entrance just as we squeezed through.

Running full-tilt downhill, Sam reached for my hand. I clasped him tightly and we darted into the first side street that we came to. Passing several buildings, I heard the carriage finally move out of the way and footsteps pounded on the cobblestones. "Quickly, jump through there," I said, pointing at a window. None of the windows in hell had glass, so we didn't have to smash our way inside. Only the carriages seemed to have glass. It was probably to keep the dirt out during travelling.

Pushing Sam ahead of me, I dived through the opening and into a dusty room. A table and a few chairs were the only furniture. They were made of the same petrified black wood as the door. Sam took my hand and we hurried out into the hallway. We made our way through to the front door. It faced a narrow, winding pathway and we darted along it to another building.

Entering through doors and windows of buildings at random, we crept away from the palace until we could no longer hear pursuit. We finally stopped for a rest inside a shabby little building and sat down on hard, uncomfortable chairs. Most of the houses that we'd passed through had been empty. Whoever lived in them was hard at work somewhere. They were either lugging stone around to make repairs on the buildings, or they were possibly torturing souls.

"How is your back?" Sam asked.

"It's healed already, but I'd like to know how my jacket is." I turned around so he could examine my back. I'd felt the wound close some time ago and only hoped my jacket would also magically repair itself again.

"Your beloved jacket is fine," he said.

I turned back in time to see him rolling his eyes. "I guess sneaking into the palace is out now that they know we're here," I said morosely.

"How are we going to kill the Prince and find the object that he is guarding if we cannot even get into his home?"

Morax had an answer and spoke into my mind. *One of the lesser demons believes there is a secret way into the palace.*

And he's only offering this information now? My response was laced with annoyance. *Where is this secret entrance?*

He has heard that there is a tunnel that leads to the top of the hill. It is rumored to be hidden somewhere in the pit.

I didn't like the sound of that at all. *What pit?*

It is where the souls are kept and where they are tortured. It is on the outskirts of the city.

Okay, I guess we'll have to go and check it out. Not that we had much choice about that if we wanted to get into the palace. "I have good news and bad news," I said to Sam.

"I take it your legion had information for you?" He'd recognized the intent look on my face. It was the one I always had when I was talking to the voices inside my head.

"Yep. Morax says there might be a tunnel that leads to the palace. The downside is that it's in the pit where the souls are being kept."

He didn't look very happy to hear that. "While it is good that we have a solution to our problem, I fear this will not be a pleasant way for us to enter the Prince's domain."

Chapter Twenty-Nine

It wasn't difficult to find the pit. We just had to follow the moans of anguish and shrieks of pain. They came from near the gate where we'd entered the city. There was no north, south, east or west here. Left, right and up and down were the only directions that seemed to apply in hell.

Sneaking around without being detected was even harder now that the demons knew we were here. Gargoyles circled overhead as they scoured the city for us. The light was pallid and cast their shadows faintly on the cobbled streets.

Sam kept us camouflaged as often as possible. We ducked into vacant buildings every time we encountered lesser demons. They were out in force, searching for us. I was pretty sure their intent was to kill rather than to capture. The Hellmaster might want me alive, but the Demon Princes wanted me dead. With their leader right here to punish them if they failed, the minions were wise to obey him rather than the master of hell. He was most likely far away somewhere in the first realm.

We made our way to the wall that enclosed the city and climbed over it. I paused at the top for a moment when I saw the pit. All I saw was a large black hole before I dropped to the ground. It wasn't safe to linger and gawk. Too many gargoyles had taken to the skies and they could stray in our direction at any time

The edge of the pit was only a short distance away. Up this close, the noise was overwhelming. It was too deep to see inside, but we'd be getting a closer view very shortly.

Hunching over so we were low to the ground, we crept to the edge to peer downward. The pit was vast and it was crammed from wall to wall with souls. On their knees, they were naked and were chained together. Their skin had turned midnight black once they'd been sent here. They were hideous and twisted from all the sins that they'd committed.

It seemed that the worse their sins had been, the greater their torture became. Lesser demons walked among the throng, dispensing hell's form of justice. They took great delight in spearing their charges with tridents, spears and swords. They weren't the glowing weapons they used in battle. Instead, they were rusty and cruelly barbed. I saw limbs being severed, guts pulled out and throats slit. Wailing in torment, the souls healed, only to be gored all over again.

Word hadn't yet spread to the pit that we were on the loose. The demons didn't look up to check for intruders. It was a long drop to the bottom and there was only one way down. Two soldiers guarded the only ladder. They wore leather armor rather than the sackcloth that the lower level lackeys were forced to wear.

"It will be painful and we will most likely be injured if we drop over the side," Sam whispered, "but at least we will heal."

I grimaced to show him what I thought of that, but we didn't have a choice. "Can you see the tunnel that Morax was talking about?" It was too gloomy and crowded with souls for me to make out the far edges of the pit.

He squinted as he peered into the pit and shook his head. "I cannot see any openings in the wall."

His eyesight was better than mine, but I wasn't ready to give up yet. I mentally crossed my fingers that the secret entrance would be an illusion that I would be able to see through once we were closer. "We'd better get down there before we're seen," I said and sat down on the edge of the pit. Sam took my hand and joined me. We shared a look of trepidation, then pushed ourselves off.

Sliding down the slick rock, I braced myself for impact as the ground rushed up at us. I hadn't realized just how densely packed the souls were. I landed squarely on one and flattened him. Sam landed on two and they let out surprised shrieks. Instead of breaking my legs as I'd expected to, I merely suffered some bruising. The poor creatures that had saved us from compound fractures wailed. They probably thought that this was a new form of torment.

A ripple effect spread outwards, alerting their torturers that something had happened. They turned in our direction, but Sam had already yanked me backwards. We put our backs to the wall and he merged us with it until we were almost invisible.

Two of the lesser demons pushed and shoved their way towards us. They used their weapons freely on the souls, hacking and slicing at random until they reached the epicenter of the disturbance. They didn't know what had caused the fuss, but they swung their blades around with apparent glee.

Sam tugged on my hand to get me into motion and we slowly crept away. The souls were too wrapped up in their never-ending torment to even notice us brushing past them as we made our way around the wall of the pit. With Sam leading the way, I didn't notice the secret passage until we were right on top of it. Seeing a doorway suddenly appear, I pulled him to a stop. The illusion that the wall was solid was ruined by a faint shimmer that he didn't even notice.

Much taller and wider than normal, the door was large enough for a Demon Prince to be able to use as an emergency escape. I put my hand on the knob, but it wouldn't turn. It was locked, but I knew a rune that would open it. Turning Sam around so his back was to me, I kept one hand on his arm as I opened the backpack and rummaged around inside. The container of blood was still tightly secured. I took it and one of the brushes out and went to work.

Sam kept his hand on my shoulder and his other hand on the wall to maintain our illusion. When I'd finished painting the symbol on the door, I used my teeth to tear a small wound in my palm. Surrounded by souls and their torturers, I couldn't risk pulling my dagger to cut myself. The glow would be seen across the entire pit. Speaking of the glow, the rune would give us away the moment that I activated it. We would have to move fast so we wouldn't get caught.

Checking that none of the guards or torturers were looking in our direction, I braced myself for action. "Ready?" I whispered to Sam.

"Ready," he replied.

I pressed my palm on the symbol and scarlet light bloomed. This time, the knob turned easily and I shoved the door open. The closest souls blanched when the rune flared to life. They wailed loudly, drawing the attention of their punishers. Pushing Sam ahead of me, I pulled my dagger. As I'd expected, it instantly began to glow. I scraped it over the rune before darting inside. The crimson light from the rune was already dying before I slammed the door shut.

I'd caught a glimpse of the lesser demons and the guards before the door had closed. None of them had been making their way over to us through the throng. I was pretty sure we'd managed to get inside without being seen by them. It was doubtful that the souls of the former humans would be able to tattle on us. The only sounds they were capable of making were moans and screams. Only a hellscribe would be able to gain entry once I'd broken the rune. It would be hidden behind the illusion that was masking the door from view.

It was completely dark inside the long, wide tunnel, but the legion gave me a form of night vision. The rocky ceiling was high enough for the prince to be able to walk along without scraping his horns on it. Cloven hoof prints in the dirt floor indicated that the ruler of the seventh realm had used the tunnel at some stage in the past.

I could see about a hundred yards along the tunnel. It curved upwards and to the left, presumably heading towards the palace. We started walking and the tunnel began to turn upwards at a steeper angle. It was a gradual climb and we passed smaller side tunnels every now and then. They were barely higher than my knees and looked as if they'd been dug out by animals. The air was musty and unpleasant.

Sam pointed out a different set of footprints that had strange drag marks between them. We shared a glance. They'd been made by something with pads and claws rather than hooves or shoes. "Rats?" I said out loud and he nodded. "Great," I muttered beneath my breath. Even though they'd been able to bite and claw us, the hellrats that we'd faced in the shadowlands had only been an illusion. The ones hiding in these tunnels would be very real.

Hearing a squeaking noise echo through the passageway, I froze. It sounded almost questioning. An answering squeak came from somewhere else. We heard the patter of multiple feet and the slither of tails heading towards us.

Sam pulled me back against the wall and masked us from sight. A pack of twenty or so rats appeared from a side tunnel. A second pack about the same size joined them from the opposite side. Meeting in the main passageway, they seemed to confer, then turned towards us. Their noses were twitching in overdrive. Sam might be able to mask our appearance, but he couldn't do anything to hide our scent.

We remained still as the gigantic rodents crept towards us. Knee high, their black fur was matted. I couldn't believe they could smell us over their own stench. Unlike the ravens and nags, these things weren't undead. They'd been created in hell rather than being brought here and they were very much alive.

Their noses led them straight to us, but they couldn't distinguish us from the rock wall. When it was only inches away from me, one of them stretched its head out and bumped into my shin. It gave a startled squeak and reacted the same way that any wild animal would by biting me.

Taking out a chunk of flesh along with my jeans, the smell of my blood incited hunger in the milling pack. They surged forward and carried Sam away from me. The moment our hands lost contact, I became visible. Wild squeals of rage and triumph rang out. I pulled my dagger again and it blazed with light. I'd need a better weapon to fight this many foes. At that thought, it transformed into the double bladed axe that Morax loved so much.

Fighting rats was easy compared to some of the things that I'd encountered in hell. The blade cut through them easily, leaving chopped up body parts behind as I carved my way through the pack. Unlike the gnome-like creatures that I'd fought in the eighth realm, the rodents weren't intelligent enough to understand that they were doomed. They kept coming no matter how many of them fell.

Apart from receiving a few scratches and bites, I was relatively unharmed when the last rodent went down. Sam's steak knife was bloody and he was panting from the effort of defending himself. He had claw and teeth marks on his arms and legs, but he'd heal soon enough. "I hate rats," he said with heartfelt loathing.

"These ones aren't exactly cute and cuddly." Not that the rats on Earth were particularly pleasant to be around either.

Now that the battle was over, my weapon returned to its usual form of a dagger and the glow died. I didn't need to clean it when I was in the supernatural world. The blood and guts magically disappeared after every battle. Sam didn't have the same luck and used his shirt to wipe his knife clean.

I wished that was the only battle we'd have to face, but I knew there would be others. Even now, I could hear the shuffling of feet and quiet squeaking as more rodents closed in on us.

Chapter Thirty

By the time we worked our way to the top of the long, curving tunnel, we'd encountered three more large packs of rats. We left their broken, bloodied bodies where they lay. There were too many corpses to try to hide them all. Besides, no one had used the tunnel in years. It was doubtful that anyone would stumble across the bodies and realize that we'd infiltrated the palace.

Finally reaching a large door at the end of the tunnel, we crept up to it and pressed our ears against the cold black wood. I could hear muffled voices on the other side, but I couldn't make out what they were saying. It sounded like two demons and their tone seemed almost panicked.

"This is bad," Sam said in a low voice when the voices finally stopped. His hearing was good enough to have been able to make out their words.

"Who were they and what were they saying?"

"They were two minions and they were gossiping about their Prince. He has ordered his lords to dismember a demon every minute until we are found and brought before him."

"So? Won't they just be sent back to the first realm and heal?"

"Not if the pieces are kept apart. They need to be in contact to become whole again. Knowing the fate that they will face will make them very eager to locate us."

"I don't get why they don't just rise up and overthrow him."

"He is their ruler. They must obey his every command."

"Why?"

"He has dominion over them, due to the level of power that he has gained through his conquests. You exhibited the same control when you ordered two lesser demons to fight you."

"That wasn't me," I argued. "It was Morax and the other Demon Lords."

"If you say so," he said in a doubtful tone.

It disturbed me that he thought I had that kind of influence over hell spawn. Having evil essence inside me didn't make me one of them. At least, I hoped it didn't. My face appearing on the carriage contradicted that hope, but I pushed the thought away. I couldn't deal with the implications of what might be happening to me right now.

This door was locked as well, which wasn't a surprise. I painted the rune on it, trying not to gag at the smell of the demon blood. My dagger sliced into my palm and I activated the symbol. I didn't hear shouts coming from the other side, so hopefully no one had been close enough to feel the flare of unholy power that I'd just used. The lords were more attuned to the black magic than the lesser demons were.

I couldn't hear any movement through the door and pulled it open a crack. A long, wide hallway stretched out ahead with another one angling to the right. A lone guard stood in front of a door to the right, but he was looking in the opposite direction. I stepped out and Sam followed me. As soon as I pulled the door shut, the illusion that it was just a blank wall returned.

It was oppressive being in the hallway with slick black rock on every surface. Flaming torches had been added every fifty yards or so. They did little to illuminate the halls, but they added to the creepy atmosphere.

Five lesser demons dressed in black sackcloth rounded the corner far to the right. Sam had already made us blend into the wall. We shuffled closer to see they were carrying severed body parts. Reaching the door where the guard was on duty, they waited impatiently for him to open it. They tossed the heads and limbs inside, then he closed the door again. They couldn't quite hide their disturbed expressions at the shuffling, shimmying sounds that were coming from within the room.

"Eww," I whispered. "They must be keeping the body parts in different rooms so they don't become reattached."

"That is sick, even for a Demon Prince," Sam replied just as quietly.

"We need to find his chambers. If we're lucky, he's keeping the object there." Something told me we wouldn't be that fortunate, but we had to at least search for it.

Turning away from the room where the dismembered demon pieces were being kept, we followed the hallway to the corner. Glassless windows lined the wall on our left. I glanced outside to see the gloomy city below. Lesser demons and soldiers swarmed through the streets, still desperately searching for us. Gargoyles flew overhead, eyes scanning the ground for anything suspicious. They didn't realize that we'd broken into the palace yet. I wanted us to remain unnoticed for as long as possible.

We passed several doors until we reached the next corner. A second guard stood outside a room where we could hear the disturbing sounds of body parts moving around.

An archway with a set of stairs leading upwards was only a few yards away from the guard. With Sam merging us with the wall, we crept towards the archway and froze when we heard footsteps clomping down. A pair of Demon Lords emerged a few moments later. They passed by us so closely that I had to shuffled my feet back so my toes didn't get squished.

"This constant dismemberment has to stop," one of the lords said. She looked back over her shoulder to make sure the guard couldn't hear her.

"I would like to see you tell our Prince that," her companion replied slyly. "He would strip you of your power and banish you back to the first realm for your impertinence. I am sure there are many ambitious captains who would leap at the chance to take your place."

I'd heard that a demon who was defeated in battle, or by a hellgate during the trials, was sent back to the first realm, but it was news to me that they were also stripped of their power. That meant they'd have to conquer the gates all over again to be able to escape to Earth. I filed that knowledge away as we scurried up the stairs.

The second level of the palace was slightly smaller than the first. It was a large, square building with a hallway that stretched along the entire outer edges. We didn't venture further into the palace through any of the doorways. Our goal was to get to the prince's chambers, not to explore the place. I was hoping he'd hidden the object somewhere inside his bedroom. If he wasn't there, we would search the room for it. If he was there, I'd have to deal with him and somehow get him to tell me where it was.

Finding the stairs to the third level, we didn't

encounter any servants or guards this time. Smaller than the lower two floors, the third floor had only a few doors on the inner walls. None of them were guarded, but we could hear voices coming from deeper inside the palace.

We walked through the halls until we found the wide staircase that led to the central tower and to the prince's private retreat. The beacon was at the tip of the tower high above us. I knew from past experience that the stairs didn't reach all the way to the top of the spire. The beacon could only be reached by someone who had wings.

At the top of the long, winding staircase, we came to a short hallway where a gigantic black door awaited. Like the hallways downstairs, this one was lined with windows on each side. Hearing a piercing shriek, I peered outside to see a pair of gargoyles fighting in midair. They bit and clawed at each other while freefalling. They split apart and their wings flared out to halt their fall just before they would have splattered against the wall of the palace. Glaring in hatred, they gave up on their battle and flew in opposite directions.

Unconcerned by their display of rivalry, Sam kept close to my side as we hurried to the end of the hallway. We pressed our ears against the door and couldn't hear movement on the other side. There wasn't a large gap beneath the door that I could peer through this time. Hoping for the best, I took a deep breath, turned the knob and pushed the door open.

I froze when I saw a dozen Demon Lords standing in a semi-circle in front of me. Then a gigantic hand reached out and grabbed me by the throat and lifted me off the ground. The prince of the realm stepped into view. His hideous face was covered in the same symbols that marked his body. Twin horns flowed upwards and swept backwards over his head. The tips curved together at the end, but didn't quite meet.

"So, this is the fabled Hellscourge," he said with a sneer. His voice was deep, guttural and difficult to understand. He examined me like I was an interesting bug that was pinned to a board. "How disappointing. You are not nearly as impressive as I'd expected." His scarlet eyes flicked to Sam. My friend was cowering in fear, yet held his steak knife ready to try to rescue me. "Pull the imp's arms and legs off," the prince said. "Throw him in with the rest of the body parts."

Struggling to breathe, I managed to utter a word as I pulled my dagger. "Run!" I heard Sam's feet move into action as he bolted back down the hallway. Half of the Demon Lords took off after him.

"What do you plan to do with that pitiful thing?" the prince asked in amused derision at the weapon that was clutched in my hand. "Are you going to trim my talons for me?"

My head was swimming from a lack of air and I was on the verge of passing out. Morax shoved his way forward, taking over my body. I took a mental step backwards as he transformed the dagger into his favorite double bladed axe. My foe's amusement fled and he dropped me in surprise.

"I was thinking more along the lines of chopping your head off with it," Morax said through me. Then his axe spun into action.

Chapter Thirty-One

My axe swung towards the prince's face, but one of the lords intercepted it with his own weapon. Metal met metal with a loud clang and bright red sparks flew. The prince drew back to watch as his lieutenants dealt with me. Another one stepped up and the other four kept watch as I tried not to get hacked or stabbed to death.

Morax hadn't lied when he'd told me he was the most skilled lord in hell. He was only one step below his own prince and he easily bested these two. Exchanging glances, the other four lords all called on their various weapons and rushed me at once.

Using my body as a puppet, Morax danced, ducked and wove his way through them. I was much smaller than they were, but he didn't let my size difference get in the way. My axe cleaved into my enemies, leaving terrible wounds that stole their lives. My touch meant death and no demon was powerful enough to survive it.

I was sporting a few cuts and slices, but was relatively unharmed when I turned to face the prince. My wounds healed quickly, leaving no trace of scars behind. Proving he wasn't the sporting type, his massive blade was already whooshing towards my face. Morax spun away, but he wasn't quite fast enough. Pain flared as my right cheek was sliced open.

Blood sheeted down to drip from my jaw, but I could already feel it healing. The prince's confident grin faltered when he saw the wound close. "That is not possible," he grated in his guttural voice. "You are just a lowly human."

I'd had this debate before and I wasn't about to indulge in it again. Repetition tended to bore me. My rage had flared along with the pain of being wounded. Morax was forced into the background as I allowed the anger to take over. "You have incurred my wrath, Prince of the seventh realm," I said and his face turned ashen. He knew the prophecy as well as any demon. "I am going to take your life. It's up to you whether your death will be quick and painless, or if it will be long and drawn out."

His forked tongue flicked out as he licked his lips nervously. He shifted his grip on his broadsword and his eyes moved to the doorway beyond me. They turned sly and I sensed danger a moment before a spear skewered me. I looked down to see a crimson blade protruding from my chest. It was yanked out and I went down to my knees. The pain was excruciating. One of my lungs had been punctured and I could hear a whistling sound inside me with each labored breath that I took. It had missed my heart by only a fraction.

"And so the mighty Hellscourge has fallen," the prince gloated. "Taken down by a minor demon, no less. I am afraid that the tales about you were wildly blown out of proportion."

He stepped in front of me and raised his sword over his head with both arms. He was going to split me straight down the middle. He didn't realize that my wound had already healed. My weapon changed to a sword and I lunged forward to skewer him in the stomach. Replicating what the Wraith Warrior had done to me, I yanked the blade sideways, slicing a wide gash in his flesh and scrambling his insides. Bellowing in agony, the prince dropped his sword. It landed on the floor behind him with a deafening clang as he dropped to his knees.

I stood and we were face to face even though he was still on his knees. Shuffling footsteps behind me reminded me that we weren't alone. I spun around and my sword decapitated the lesser demon before she could stab me again. The Demon Prince was desperately trying to hold his guts in, but disgusting black things similar to intestines were slithering out through the gash. The wound was too catastrophic even for someone as powerful as him to be able to heal easily.

I prodded him in the chest with my sword tip and he flinched. "Are you responsible for sending the Wraith Warrior after me?"

He looked surprised for a moment, then bared his teeth in a bloody grin. "It was not I, but I wish I could claim it was so. If you have been marked, then your death is inevitable."

My rage surged up again, but I didn't give into it yet. I had two more questions that I needed to find the answers for. "Why are the Collectors harvesting souls and where do they take them?"

Swaying on his knees, his strength was rapidly fading. He was doomed, but he fought against the darkness that was coming to steal his life. "I do not know. Our new master keeps that knowledge to himself."

I had one final question and knew I was running out of time. "Where is your piece of the object of power?"

His upper lip lifted in a sneer, showing his ivory colored fangs. "I will never tell you what I have done with it."

"Wrong answer," I replied and shoved the sword into him, making him roar in fresh agony.

Several stabs later, he held up his hand in defeat. "Stop! I will tell you what you wish to know." He'd given up on trying to hold onto his guts. They'd slithered out of him a while ago, around the same time that he'd lost the strength to stay on his knees. He lay on his back now and I had to step delicately around his entrails as I searched for a new place to stab him.

"Well?" I prompted when he didn't speak.

Gasping for breath, he lifted his head weakly. "I had the object thrown into a forbidden place where no one dares to enter." Even though he was dying, he still managed a sly grin. "Not even you will be able to retrieve it and return unscathed."

"Where is this place?" I asked, but his face had frozen in the creepy grin. Black blood had pooled around him, spreading out in a wide puddle. I hadn't even had the chance to end him myself. He'd bled to death instead.

Footsteps approached me from behind. I turned to see the six Demon Lords who had sprinted after Sam returning. They stared at their fallen leader in shock. "Where is my friend?" I asked.

"He is all over the place by now," one of them snarled nastily. "We have ordered his pieces to be scattered throughout the palace. You will never be able to find all of his body parts."

My fury rose again and I didn't need Morax's help this time. I ran at them and they turned to flee. My sword changed back into an axe. It sliced through their legs, cutting two of them down. The other four tried to look over their shoulders and run at the same time. Tripping, they fell over each other and clattered to the floor.

I leaped among them, slicing and hacking until they were still. The other two had dragged themselves backwards, but they hadn't made it far. Their scarlet eyes pleaded with me for mercy, but I didn't have that capacity when I was this enraged. I ended their lives, then fell to my knees in a puddle of sticky blood. Holding onto my sobs, I tried to get myself under control. Sam was an imp, which meant that he was immortal. They'd hinted that he would be able to piece himself back together if I could just gather up his parts. All I had to do was search every room in the palace until I found all of him.

"Piece of cake," I croaked. How the hell was I supposed to tell his body parts apart from the others? His flesh was more ash gray than black now, but it would still be almost indistinguishable from a demon's when it was all hacked up.

"What is a piece of cake?" a familiar voice asked from behind me. Whirling around, I saw Sam standing there, completely intact.

Lurching to my feet, I leaped over the bloody corpses and wrapped my arms around him. "They said they hacked you to pieces," I said.

"They lied," he replied. "Demons have a tendency to do that."

I laughed, but it turned into tears and I sobbed on his shoulder in utter relief. The thought of losing Sam had almost torn me apart. He was more than just my best friend. He was also my guide through hell. Without him, there was no way I'd be able to survive long enough to kill the remaining six princes, then hunt down their master.

"There, there," he said awkwardly as he patted my back in comfort. "I am fine."

Finally regaining control, I pushed myself away and glanced over my shoulder. The prince seemed to be mocking me as he lay dead on the floor of his bedroom. "We should get out of here before anyone comes to check on him."

"His lackeys are a little busy at the moment. They are still carrying on with the dismemberments," Sam said with a grimace as he took the lead. I kept my hand on his shoulder and he trailed his hand along the wall as we headed downstairs. He was ready to camouflage us if we saw or heard anyone approaching.

"I'm sure they'll stop once they realize their leader is dead. They'll probably throw a party in my honor."

I could hear the doubt in his tone when he replied. "That is unlikely. I expect that they will instead flee in terror when they learn of his demise."

"Then they'll probably set the hounds on us again," I said morosely. "We need to get back to the secret entrance before they turn up and start searching for us."

"Did you find the object?" he asked as we reached the end of the stairs and stepped out into the hallway.

"Nope. The Prince said he had it thrown into a forbidden place where no one dares to go, whatever that means."

"We should ask someone who might know the answer," he proposed.

"Good idea. We'll grab the next lesser demon that we come across and question them."

Chapter Thirty-Two

We kept close to the wall and backtracked to the staircase that led to the second floor. Just as Sam had told me, dismembered pieces of lesser demons were still being carried to the rooms where the parts were being stored.

Lying in wait, we saw a lone minion coming and got ready. Her arms were full, so we let her continue on. When she returned, I leaped forward and slapped my hand over her mouth while Sam opened the door at our back. I dragged her into the room and he shut the door. "Be quiet, or I'll kill you," I whispered with my dagger pressed against her throat.

She twisted around enough to see my face and realized who I was. She nodded frantically in agreement and I let her go. "What do you want with me?" she said in a near wail and spun around to face me. "I am just a lowly servant."

"Shh!" I put a finger to my lips and she clapped a hand over her mouth in fear. "Have you heard of a forbidden place where no one dares to go?"

Her face screwed up in confusion for a moment before her expression cleared. "You mean the swamp where a city once stood?" she asked in a hoarse whisper.

I nodded, pretending I knew what she was talking about. "Where is it?"

"I do not know," she said with a frightened shrug. "No one has been there in eons. Not since the ground turned to marsh and destroyed most of the buildings."

"That's just great. How are we going to find it?" I said to Sam.

"The nightmares will probably know where it is," he reminded me.

"Oh yeah. I forgot about them."

The servant's eyes had grown wide. "Nightmares obey your summons?" she said incredulously.

"Why wouldn't they?" I asked. "I defeated the master gate, so I'm entitled to use them whenever I need to travel somewhere."

"It does not work that way," she said in flat denial. "No human has the power to command the creatures of hell."

"Then I guess the Demon Lords that are floating around inside me must be how I manage to pull it off."

Horror stole across her face as she realized what I meant. She let out a piercing shriek at the thought of her soul being added to my collection. She had no way of knowing that I couldn't ingest her essence here, but the damage was already done. Feet pounded down the hallway towards us.

We darted over to the door that was on the other side of the room, wincing at her shrill screams. We ran through a confusing labyrinth of hallways and rooms until we reached a balcony. I peered over the edge to see the throne room far below.

Demons were reluctantly crowded in together to witness the dismemberments that were still being carried out. We watched as a lesser demon was dragged forward. He was pinned to the ground, screaming and thrashing as his arms and legs were chopped off. His body was hacked into two pieces and then his head was lopped off. His screams ended, but he was still alive as he was carried off in different directions.

I wasn't sure why the injured lackeys didn't simply go back to the first realm. Maybe because, although they were in pieces, they weren't badly damaged enough to be banished. Trust the demons to find a loophole that they could exploit.

Feeling sick to my stomach, I didn't protest when Sam pulled me down the hallway. We managed to find our way to the stairs and blended in with the stone as we hurried downward.

Panic was beginning to spread as word got out that

I was in the building. A roar went up when the prince's body was discovered. We stayed close to the wall when a flood of demons entered the wide passageway. The exodus had begun and we just had to wait for the palace to empty out so we could leave.

Following the fleeing minions at a slower pace, I found the door that led to the hidden passageway. I reached out, but the knob wouldn't turn. I'd unlocked it from the other side, but it looked like I'd now have to draw the rune again to unlock it from this side.

"Hurry," Sam urged me when the first hollow howl rang out. The hellhounds had been released and they were already hunting for us.

He opened the backpack and reached for the container of blood. He held it for me as I dipped a brush into the thick, clotted mixture. Working quickly, I painted a reverse copy of the symbol that was on the other side.

A low growl came from behind us and echoed along the hallway. We turned to see three hellhounds approaching at a run. Three more started sprinting towards us from the other corridor. I tried to remain calm as I sliced my palm open and slapped my hand on the rune to activate it. I opened the door and we ducked through and slammed it shut just as the hounds reached us. I hadn't had time to break the rune, which meant the door could be opened again. Everyone would be able to see it now that I'd broken the enchantment that had kept it hidden.

"Do you think the hounds are smart enough to

figure out how to turn the doorknob?" I asked as we started running downhill.

"I do not know, but I sincerely hope not," Sam replied.

We'd been running for a few minutes when we heard the howls start up inside the tunnel. Either one of the hounds had accidentally managed to turn the knob, or someone had opened the door for them.

From the number of howls, more than one pack was after us now. Their feet made no noise on the soil, but their barks, yips and howls echoed around us. We increased our speed until we were running flat out. Our foes were much faster than us and the hellhounds quickly gained ground.

I cast a look back over my shoulder to see the scarlet glow from their eyes lighting up the darkness. They were just around the bend and would see us in moments. Sam caught hold of my hand and pulled me down to my knees. He didn't bother to explain what he was doing, but merely disappeared inside one of the smaller tunnels that had been made by the rats.

Seeing how tiny the opening was, I froze in fear. Claustrophobia clawed at me and I couldn't bring myself to move forward. *Now is not the time to succumb to your childish terror,* Morax scolded me. When he realized that I was incapable of entering the tunnel, he took matters into his own hands.

I tried to scream as he forced me into the rat hole, but he clamped my mouth shut. There wasn't enough room for me to crawl, so he flattened me down to my belly. Sam was just ahead of me, looking back over his shoulder. Not realizing that I wasn't following him voluntarily, he gave me a thumbs up.

He slithered through the soil and Morax forced me after him. We halted when a howl sounded from right outside the tiny tunnel. I peered backwards to see several packs of midnight black hounds with red glowing eyes sprint past the opening. Morax motioned for Sam to keep going and I slithered after him.

Shunted to the back of my own mind, I gibbered in terror at being in such a tightly confined space. The memory of being trapped in the toy chest when I'd been a toddler returned with a vengeance.

You're safe, Violet, a voice said inside my head. It was Heather. She'd left the home that I'd constructed for her to keep her safe from the demons. My terror had drawn her out.

You are not alone, Hellscourge, Sy said. The hellscribe had also left the house to offer me what comfort he could. Mentally clutching at both of them, I could almost feel them holding my hands as Morax continued to propel me along.

We headed downhill, taking what turned out to be a shortcut through the center of the hill beneath the palace. The rats had chewed their way through the black rock that lined the main passageway. All we had to do was keep going down and we'd eventually reach the exit.

I had a few moments of relief when we emerged

into the main hallway, but Sam quickly entered the much smaller tunnels again. Somewhere in the distance, the howls changed in tone and became frustrated.

"The hounds have realized that the trail they are following is not fresh," Sam said as he pulled himself along on his elbows and knees. Our hands, faces and clothes were filthy.

"I believe they are backtracking in an attempt to find us," Morax said through my mouth. I was in no shape to respond to Sam.

"You do not sound like yourself," my best friend said suspiciously.

"Hellscourge is currently indisposed," the Demon Lord replied in a dry tone. "The tunnels are too small for her to bear."

Sam sent a stricken look at me over his shoulder. "I forgot about her claustrophobia. Is she okay?"

"No. She is cowering inside her own mind so she does not have to deal with her terror." Morax heaved a put-upon sigh for having to shoulder the task of using my body. "I do not understand how she can be so powerful, yet at the same time so pitifully weak."

"That is because you were never human," Sam said in my defense. "You do not have the same capacity to feel emotion that they do."

"The longer I spend inside her head, the more I understand just how driven by emotion humans are. It is no wonder they are so easily tempted to sin." He sounded so smug that I was almost pulled out of my misery to respond.

When he reached the next exit that led to the main tunnel, Sam waited for me to emerge behind him then started sprinting. Morax retreated and I was thrust back into the front of my own mind again. I stumbled a step, but Sam caught my arm. "I take it you are back now?"

"Yeah," I replied raggedly. "Let's try to avoid going into any small, dark spaces again."

"I am sorry I put you through that."

His guilt was evident, but I waved it away. "Don't worry about it. Let's just concentrate on getting out of here." It hadn't been pleasant to take the shortcut, but it had been clever. We now had a lead on the hounds and it would be smart to utilize it.

Even the wide tunnel was too enclosed for me after the harrowing ordeal of being forced to slither through the rat holes. When I spied the door that led to freedom just ahead, gladness surged through me.

My hands were shaking too much for me to try to paint the rune this time. I talked Sam through it instead. He did a respectable job of marking out the symbol. He took my dagger from me and made a small incision on my palm. I placed my hand on the rune and it flared to life.

Far behind us, the hounds were still confused about where we'd disappeared to. Maybe the scent of the rats drowned out our smell. It had been pretty rank moving through their lair.

Pulling the door open, I was almost knocked off

my feet by strong wind. I looked up to see dark, ominous clouds forming over the pit. "Uh oh," I said and Sam crowded in beside me to see. "I think the Hellmaster knows that the Prince is dead."

The last time I'd killed one of his lieutenants, he'd sent lightning after us. This time, it looked like he'd sent a tornado.

Chapter Thirty-Three

It might just be a show the master of hell was putting on for the benefit of his minions, but the storm was very real. The ominous clouds began to spin as the tornado picked up speed. I was torn between braving the elements, and staying put in the tunnel. Wild baying and hollow howls as the hounds picked up our scent again dissuaded me from that idea. Morax was a fearsome fighter, but not even he could take on thirty or so hounds without sustaining severe injuries.

I decided that I'd rather be torn to pieces by a gigantic whirlwind than to hide from the hellhounds in one of the cramped tunnels again. "Come on," I said to Sam and pushed him outside. I scraped my dagger across the rune to lock it from the inside, then stepped out and struggled to pull the door shut. It took both of us fighting against the wind before we managed to get it closed.

Sam kept hold of me as we made our way past the moaning, wailing souls. Loose dirt was being drawn into the vortex that was growing stronger by the second. Lesser demons were pointing up at it in confusion. Weather was an unknown phenomenon to them. This was the first tornado to ever occur in hell and they had no idea what to do.

The souls were far more familiar with the repercussions of the storm. They covered their heads with their hands and tried to flatten themselves down. Sam kept his back to the wall as he sidled towards the ladder and I copied him. My hand was clutched in his tightly as we hurried as fast as we could around the thick press of souls.

Two soldiers still guarded the only escape route, not that any of the souls had a hope of being able to flee. They were tightly chained to each other, which would have made it hard for them to climb. The guards stared up at the roiling clouds in awe that was tinged with fear.

Wind plucked at me with insistent invisible fingers, inviting me to play. It was an invitation that I wasn't about to accept. It grew stronger, snatching at me now with greedy hands. Sam lurched forward and grabbed hold of the ladder just as the tornado descended and havoc ensued.

The chains that were holding the souls together snapped as if they were made out of paper. Their bodies were sucked up into the vortex. Lesser demons desperately tried to run and had nowhere to run to. Sam hauled me towards him and I held onto the ladder with a panicked grip. The two guards saw us, but were torn away before they could react to our presence.

Looking up, I saw the epicenter of the tornado high above us. It had spread out to cover part of the city as well. Gargoyles that flew too close to the unnatural disaster were drawn into the vortex. Whirling around and around, they were spat out to fall to the ground far below.

My feet left the ground and my hair whipped around me wildly as the wind did its best to pluck me off the ladder. Sam held onto me grimly with his legs wrapped around the rungs. His expression told me that he would never let me go, no matter how badly the Hellmaster wanted to punish me for killing another one of his princes.

Either running out of power, or realizing that I wasn't going to be pulled into its clutches so easily, the tornado finally began to lose steam. The clouds stopped spinning and the wind died down. Sam motioned me to start climbing and I didn't need to be urged twice.

Once the tornado began to wane, bodies started to rain from the sky. Souls and lesser demons alike splattered on the hard ground. The human souls remained, but their torturers shimmered, then disappeared. They'd been so badly wounded that they'd been sent back to the first realm. They would stay there until another Demon Lord took them through a gate as part of their entourage.

Wincing at every splat that I heard, I refused to look down to see the carnage. The souls were immortal and would eventually recover their usual twisted shapes. At least their incessant wailing had finally stopped. It was eerily quiet as I finally reached the top of the ladder. I climbed off and waited for Sam to appear. Gargoyles still flew over the city, so we raced over to the wall and melded against it before we were spotted.

Demons were streaming out of the city in droves. We heard their panicked voices shouting questions at each other. Some of them weren't even sure what they were running from. Others invoked my name like a curse. The tornado had frightened them almost as much as I had. In his quest to make them believe that he was angry that the prince was dead, their ultimate ruler had alienated himself from his lackeys even further.

I waited until we were a safe distance away from the pit before I mentally called for my carriage. The nightmares appeared moments later and pranced to a halt a few yards away. We clambered inside before any of the gargoyles could arrow in on us.

Sticking my head out the window, I waited for the nightmare to turn its head before I spoke. "Stamp your hoof once if you know where the swamp that took over a city is located." It lifted its lip in a sneer, then they took off at a gallop.

Falling back onto my plush leather seat with a chuckle, I saw Sam grinning at me. "You have the strangest sense of humor of anyone that I have ever met."

"You're lucky I can still laugh about any of this. You could have ended up with some moody girl who mopes about constantly feeling sorry for herself."

Or someone who is so afraid of small spaces that they go completely insane with terror when they are forced to enter a narrow tunnel, Morax added dryly.

Who invited you into this conversation?

My snide thought didn't bother him at all. *This is the thanks I get for saving your hide from the hounds?*

I struggled with my conscience, then gave in. *Thanks.* It came out grudgingly, but it was sincere. If he hadn't stepped up and taken over my body and forced me into action, I'd have ended up as dog food. I knew he'd really just acted to save himself, but I still owed him one.

I am sure I will think of a way that you can repay me one day.

Owing a Demon Lord a favor was a disturbing prospect. Hopefully, I wouldn't have to come good on it anytime soon. The only thing he could possibly want from me was to be freed from my mind. I'd be doing us all a favor if I managed to pull that off.

As we headed across the wastelands, we regularly passed near or through villages at first. After a few hours, they became fewer and fewer until we left any trace of civilization far behind. At a guess, we'd been in hell for nearly three whole days now. I wasn't sure how much time had passed on Earth.

Sophia had told me that time passed differently here. It went faster, but actually seemed to be going slower. I just hoped we weren't gone for so long that Zach became alarmed by my absence. It would be difficult to explain where I'd disappeared to if I remained absent for too long.

I didn't feel any different yet, but I was concerned about what effect being here was having on my body. The longer a living being spent in hell, the more twisted they became. Sam was absorbed with looking out through the window, so I quickly lifted my jacket and t-shirt. I looked down at the scar that ran across my abdomen and winced. The tendrils had spread a tiny bit. I didn't feel any pain at the moment, but I was sure it would come eventually.

Chapter Thirty-Four

With nothing to do but wait until the carriage carried us to our destination, I fell into a doze. It deepened into true sleep and I was sucked into a strange dream. After a few seconds, I realized I was a passenger inside a young woman's head. She was creeping through a city that had archaic buildings that looked like they were from ancient Rome or maybe Greece. I watched through her eyes as she left the city behind. A quick peek inside her memories told me her name was Hannah. Then I became immersed as her thoughts took over.

It was dangerous to sneak out of the city at night, but the lure of meeting my love was too strong. We were betrothed to be married, but that was still several weeks away. I wanted to be joined with him now. We'd arranged to meet beneath a large tree in a nearby meadow. It was where we'd first encountered each other a year ago and it was where we would consummate our love.

Once I was free of the buildings, I ran to the meadow. The moonlight was just bright enough to illuminate the tree in the distance. I was only halfway across the field when a man appeared in front of me. He was tall and had dark hair and skin. I'd never seen him before, but something in his expression told me to be wary of him.

Before I could flee, he caught me by the arm. I tried to scream, but bright red light flared around me. When my vision cleared, the meadow was gone and had been replaced with a sandy beach. I saw a dark doorway carved into a nearby cliff face. The strange man dragged me towards it.

Tears of terror blurred my eyes and I struggled to get free, but he was too strong. He hauled me into a dark, narrow passageway that had yellow moss on the walls. He stopped after a while and his body shuddered. Black fog was expelled from him. When it solidified, a monster was staring down at me.

My mind came close to breaking and I was numb with horror. More than twice my height, he had a hideous face, large horns and cloven hooves. Most of his body was covered in black metal armor. His chest was left exposed. What I could see of his skin was marked with strange symbols.

The man that he'd hidden inside was no longer needed and he cut him down with a glowing red sword. The body fell and lay there with wide, staring eyes. I cowered when he turned his attention back to me. "You are a very beautiful woman," the creature said as he studied my face. "I have not had a human with such pale hair and green eyes before. Let us hope that you will last longer than the others."

I was a virgin, but I wasn't completely without knowledge and knew what he was referring to. Screams issued from me and I couldn't stop them. His gigantic hand came towards my face and I fainted from sheer terror.

When I woke, I was in what looked like an enclosed chariot. The monster that had captured me took up the entire seat across from mine. His horns brushed against the roof. Wings that I hadn't noticed before were tucked behind him. Although I could hear the wheels of the chariot, I couldn't hear the horses that were presumably pulling us. Their hooves made no sound at all.

I slipped in and out of consciousness and eventually woke to find myself in a circular chamber made of cold black stone. My clothing was gone and I was naked.

"Good, you are awake," a deep, guttural voice said. It was the demon who had stolen me from my beloved. "I prefer my conquests to be awake when I take them." His smile was wicked and I began to scream even before he undressed and climbed on top of me. My mind broke as he took my innocence and I went somewhere far away.

I found myself standing in a field. The grass was so long that it brushed my fingertips. Turning in a circle, I saw a hill and headed towards the top. It ended in a cliff with an ocean far below. Waves crashed on the rocks and I contemplated throwing myself over to end my misery.

"You have been chosen for an important destiny, child," a hollow voice said. I spun around to see a woman dressed in a black cloak with a hood that hid her face. She was about my height and size and seemed to be wreathed in moving shadows.

"Who are you? What do you mean?"

"I am Fate. If you agree to my request, you will be instrumental in saving the entire human race from eventual annihilation."

I struggled to understand what she was talking about. Far away, my body was on fire from pain. "What do you want from me?"

"I merely need you to survive." I could feel her studying me from the shadows of her hood. "In the distant future, one of your descendants will be in this very room, facing this Demon Prince. She will be the champion I will choose to save this world from the coming darkness."

"The demon is raping me to death even as we speak," I said bitterly. "We both know that I will not live through what he is doing to my body."

"You will live," she disagreed. "I will ensure that your body will be healed."

"And my mind?" I asked. I was already teetering on

the edge of madness. To return to wakefulness and experience what was being done to me would shred my sanity completely.

"The memory of this night will be stricken from you forever. I have arranged for you to escape and for someone to rescue you once you have left hell."

My blood tried to freeze in my veins, but I'd lost too much of it for that to be possible. I was in hell, the dreaded underworld where demons roamed free. "What do you need from me?"

"I need you to choose between life or death."

It was a simple choice, but my answer would impact on the entire world and every human who was living in it. I wanted to give up and fall into oblivion, but my conscience wouldn't let me. Drawing on a strength that I didn't know I'd possessed, I gave her my answer. "I choose life."

Her expression was hidden from me, but I felt a fierce swell of triumph coming from her. "You are strong, Hannah. Your distant progeny will be even stronger. I have made the right choice and so have you."

The dream faded and I woke to an agony so intense that I couldn't breathe. With a final groan of satisfaction, the Demon Prince finished with me. He climbed off the bed and a knock sounded at the door. "Enter," he commanded.

A hooded demon came in and slid a look at me. I didn't have the strength to try to cover my nakedness. "You wished to see me, Sire?"

"Get rid of the body," his master said as he casually cleaned himself of my blood with a cloth.

The smaller demon looked at me again and met my eyes. "I do not think she is dead yet, your highness."

Surprised, the Demon Prince spun around to stare at me. A small amount of strength flowed into me and Fate spoke with my voice. "Several eons from now, you will die at the hands of a mortal woman. You will pay for your sick, twisted crimes."

"You are not as weak as I believed," he said, dismissing my words. "Wait outside," he commanded his robed lackey.

Again, my mind slipped away as he used my body to satisfy his needs. I trusted in Fate to keep me sane and alive. She fed me her strength and cradled me through the abuse. When I woke again, I was only just clinging to life.

Nine days have passed, Fate told me. *It is time for you to escape from this realm.*

I am too weak. I doubt that I can even stand without help.

I have seen to it that you will have assistance. She fed me a little more of her strength. *Are you ready?*

I wasn't, but I took a mental breath anyway. *I am ready.*

My eyes opened to the dim light of the bedchamber. The Demon Prince lay beside me, stroking a claw down my torso. I was covered in cuts from his talons, but they were nothing compared to the other wounds that my body had suffered. He noticed that my eyes were on him and smiled slyly.

"Well, well. You are finally awake. I prefer to have your undivided attention rather than you just lying there in a coma."

Fate spoke through me. "Your bestial actions have ensured your downfall, Prince of the eighth realm of hell."

"Ah, she speaks," he said mockingly. "It is a pity that you make no sense whatsoever."

"In the distant future, a human unlike any other will be born. She will be the end of you and your fellow Princes," Fate said in her hollow voice.

The demon gave a gravelly laugh. "No mere woman will be able to defeat me, or my brothers. We have earned our places as Princes through combat. We are the strongest warriors in Satan's army."

"Satan will fall and another will take his place. He will drench the Earth in blood and fire."

His expression grew wary. He climbed out of bed and clad himself in the armor that he could draw into being as easily as he could call on his sword. "Who are you?" he asked.

"I am an agent of Fate," she replied and his skin turned ashen. Hearing footsteps approach the door, I sensed someone was listening as she spoke again. "Hear my decree; Gold of hair, green of eye and bearing two opposing natures, she shall purge the nine realms of its leaders, leaving devastation in her wake. Hellscourge shall bring death to anyone who incurs her wrath."

His brow furrowed in a dire frown at her

proclamation. "Dantanian!" he bellowed.

The door burst open and the robed demon entered. "Yes, my liege?" He bowed his head submissively.

"I am weary of bedding this female and she refuses to die like all the others. I want her to be dismembered and for her body parts scattered throughout the nine realms."

Picking up on his master's nervousness, the lackey bowed deeper. "It shall be done." He strode over to the bed and tossed the sheet over me. He bundled me over his shoulder and carried me from the room.

Dantanian didn't speak a word as he made his way along a short walkway, then down a long spiral staircase. Making his way out of the gigantic palace that was made of black stone, we entered a much smaller building that seemed to be a stable. Gray horses stared at me through milky eyes as I was deposited on the hard ground. Their bodies were thin and malnourished and they weren't breathing. I shuddered and tried to remain still, hoping they wouldn't come any closer. "Stay there," Dantanian ordered me. "Do not move." His scarlet eyes were alight with what seemed to be excitement.

He dashed away and returned a few minutes later with a demon that was taller and larger than him, but smaller than the prince. Her horns weren't as long and her body wasn't carved with runes. "Why have you brought me here, scribe?" she asked the robed lackey.

"I overheard something that I thought you should

know about," Dantanian replied. He relayed the prophecy that he'd overheard, leaving out the part that I was an agent of Fate. He either hadn't heard it, or he was keeping it to himself.

"What does this mean?" the taller female asked.

"It means that we have an opportunity to escape from this prison," the scribe replied slyly. I watched through my eyelashes, pretending to be unconscious. "When the new ruler rises," he continued, "we will be free to wreak havoc on Earth."

That prospect made the female grin. "What is your plan?" She knew he was more intelligent than she was and that his mind had been working overtime.

"We should spread rumors of the prophecy of this 'Hellscourge' to cause fear among our rivals. Meanwhile, we will keep the rest of what the witch said to ourselves. We will have to keep watch for the one who will overthrow Satan. If we pledge ourselves to him, he might make us his lieutenants. Instead of being low in the hierarchy, we can rise to positions of power."

She mulled it over, then nodded in agreement. "What do you need me to do?"

"You have only recently become a lord. I have heard that you have not yet taken an entourage through to Earth."

She eyed him mistrustfully. "It is forbidden for Hellscribes to become part of our entourage. Satan has another purpose for your kind."

"I am not the one I want you to take through the

portal." He pointed at me and the lord swiveled her head to look in my direction. "I want you to return her to where she came from."

"Why?"

"She is tied to the prophecy. I have a feeling that it is important for her to live." I had a feeling Fate had planted that idea in his head.

"Fine," the lord grumbled. "Place her in my carriage and try not to be seen."

He bundled me over his shoulder again and carried me to the wide doorway. No one was in sight, so he hurried over to the chariot that she called a carriage. It bore an image of the lord on the door. Her hideous face had been painted in extraordinary detail. The scribe opened the door and dumped me on the floor, then shut me inside and left.

Moments later, the lord climbed in with me. She kicked me over to one side where I was out of the way. Curling into a ball, I passed in and out of consciousness as we travelled. I woke briefly a sometime later as we passed through a gigantic wrought iron gate. It was ominous and almost seemed to be staring at me through the window.

We continued on until we came to a second gate after another couple of days or so had passed. I woke to hear the Demon Lord conversing with someone. "What are the rules about taking a mortal to Earth as part of my entourage?" she asked. I caught a glimpse of the gigantic gate through the curtains.

"Humans do not count," a deep male voice replied.

"Even if she did, from the state she is in I would say that she will not survive for much longer." A huge eye made of iron peered at me through the window. It appeared that the gate was somehow alive and it was responding to the lord's questions. Under normal circumstances, I would have been terrified. I'd been through too much by now to find a sentient gate particularly disturbing.

"Well then, since I recently bested you, I demand that you let us pass," the lord said haughtily.

"As you command, so it shall be done," the gate replied sarcastically. With a groaning creak, it swung open slowly.

The carriage took off again, but it was only a short journey this time. When it stopped, the lord dragged me out and threw me over her shoulder. We walked down a dark, narrow pathway and stepped out onto the beach. Then red light blazed and everything shifted. When I opened my eyes, we were standing in the field where my entire life had changed. She dropped me to the ground and I came close to passing out from pain. Without a backward glance, she disappeared.

I was unsure how long I lay there before gentle hands lifted me up. I opened my eyes to see the most beautiful man that I'd ever seen staring down at me. He had black hair that hung to his chin and dark blue eyes. His expression was conflicted as he seemed to be listening to a voice inside his head. Then he nodded and looked resigned. He placed his hand on my forehead and bliss swept through me as my wounds were healed. "Who are you?" I asked in a daze.

"You will not remember me, but my name is Nathanael," he replied. Then he faded from my sight, taking my memory of my abuse and journey to hell and back with him. I had a fleeting thought of pity for my distant relative who would be chosen by Fate to save the world. Then everything went black.

Chapter Thirty-Five

Sam put his hand on my knee, jolting me awake. For a moment, I was still lost in the memories that had happened to Hannah thousands of years ago. Fate had sent me back in time to witness what had happened to her. Now that I'd seen the events that had brought on the prophecy for myself, I knew that I was descended from her. It had been a shock to see Nathan arrive and heal her. He hadn't mentioned the part that he'd played in all this and I couldn't help but wonder why.

The Hellscribe who had been so subservient to the prince seemed to have gotten his wish. His plan to rise up from being just a lowly lackey to holding a position of power had worked. Sytry had said the Head Scribe's name was Dantanian. It just proved how clever and treacherous demons could be.

"It appears that we have arrived at our destination," Sam informed me.

Shifting the curtain aside, I looked out to see the usual desolation of the wastelands. From this angle, I couldn't see anything of interest. The carriage had stopped, so I guessed we'd gone as far as we could go via wheeled transport. "Let's see what horrors are in store for us this time," I said.

He opened the door and we both climbed out. I'd barely put my feet on the ground before the nightmares disappeared, taking the carriage with them again. "Geez, they couldn't wait to get out of here," I murmured.

Looking around at what used to be a large city, I could see why it had been abandoned. Only broken walls remained of the buildings that had most likely once housed tens of thousands of demons.

A hideous stench permeated the area. We stood at the edge of the marsh that had risen up to consume the dwellings. "Eww. That reeks," I said, putting a hand over my nose in a futile effort to block the smell. Unlike the other cities that we'd seen so far, this one didn't look like it had been built on a hill.

Sam stared at the boggy ground in distaste. We were used to the small pits that housed one or two snake-like creatures. The swamp spread as far as the eye could see, which meant the area was probably riddled with them. "I can see why the demons fled from here," he said. "Whatever caused the marsh to form had a catastrophic effect on their homes."

"It couldn't have happened to a more deserving bunch of hell spawn," I replied with a wan smile.

"I wonder if this used to be the equivalent of their capital?"

In the first two realms that we'd been to, the palace had been surrounded by large cities with smaller villages scattered around it. This was the first abandoned city that we'd seen. Peering around at the ruins, I could see a large open area in the middle. "If it was, then the palace was most likely over there." I gestured and Sam nodded. "The Prince said he had the object thrown into a place that I wouldn't be able to retrieve it from. I'm guessing it's in the middle of the ruins."

The flapping of wings drew our attention and we saw the undead raven circling overhead. It must have followed our carriage here and had only just caught up to us. It flew over the swamp and came to rest on a crumbling wall near the center of the marsh. Its caw was mocking, as if it was daring us to come closer.

I toyed with the idea of turning my dagger into a spear, but I knew the bird would fly off before I could throw it. It wasn't worth the risk of possibly losing my one and only weapon.

Although the ground was covered in sludge, I didn't think it was very deep. We could see the partial remains of buildings and I could make out the floor in some of them. The swamp had to be fairly shallow.

"I guess we'd better start searching," I said with great reluctance and stepped into the goo. As I'd suspected, it was only calf-deep. Breaking the surface had the same effect as lifting the lid on a container to let the stench out. The noisome odor became worse and rolled over us. Biting back the urge to gag, I pulled my dagger just in case. It began to glow softly, indicating that danger was near.

Sam slogged along behind me, holding his steak knife ready. His eyes searched the bog, on the lookout for threats. Tugging on my sleeve to get my attention, he pointed between two decrepit buildings. I turned to see something moving through the sludge. Arrowing towards us, it left a wake behind it that spread out to slap against the crumbling foundations. The gentle waves brought more of the snakelike creatures to investigate.

Putting on a burst of speed, I raced over to the nearest structure and leaped up onto the uneven floor. Sam scrambled up next to me and we waited for the creatures to strike. They arrowed in on us and the lead snake leaped straight up into the air. About five or six feet long, it's slimy body was covered in black scales. Its teeth were long and needle sharp. A ridge of wicked looking spines ran the length of its back. Gills opened and closed on its neck, trying to breathe air instead of sludge.

I sliced it in two and the head and body fell back into the water. More and more of them launched themselves upwards. I took as many of them down as I could until they gave up. The survivors speared off through the ooze in search of easier prey.

"That seemed a little too easy," Sam said, voicing the same concern that I had.

"I'm sure they won't be gone for long," I predicted. "They're probably going in search of backup."

The raven watched us expectantly as we slowly made our way through the quagmire. It didn't occur to me that there could be deeper holes until Sam fell into one. One second, he was walking along beside me, then he disappeared from my sight with a plop. He popped up a few seconds later, gasping for air. Panicked, he scrambled for the edge of the hole that was hidden beneath the sludge.

I felt for the hole with my foot to make sure I didn't fall in with him, then bent down and hauled him out. A snake came after him, but I kicked it away before it could latch onto his legs. Frantically wiping his face with one hand to clear the sludge out of his eyes, he brandished his knife with the other.

"Are you okay?" I asked. Usually, he was the one asking me that.

"That water tastes even more vile than it smells," he said and gagged. I wasn't sure the ooze could really be classified as water, but I was secretly glad that he'd been the one to discover the sink hole.

The disturbance had brought more of the hellsnakes. They were zooming towards us from all sides. My dagger became the axe that I was so used to now.

"Head for that building," I said and pushed him towards a nearby ruin that still had a solid floor. He slogged his way across the bog, being careful not to fall into any holes this time. Reaching the building, he jumped up onto the rocky floor.

Waiting for the snakes to close in, I spun in a circle, decapitating several of the reptiles when they leaped upwards. Splashing around in the ooze, I was soaked and reeking by the time the survivors turned tail and ran.

Changing my weapon into a spear, I prodded the ground, searching for holes as I made my way over to Sam. Covered from head to toe in muck, he looked miserable. He took the backpack off and rummaged around inside. He handed me the container of blood and several paintbrushes. Sludge poured out when he upended the backpack. It was doubtful Sophia would be able to salvage it when we returned it to her.

When the raven gave its version of a chuckle again, Sam flipped it a very human gesture that he'd picked up from watching TV.

"Do you realize you just gave a bird the bird?" I asked.

He looked surprised, then giggled. "I wish we could catch it and feed it to one of the snakes."

"We can only dream."

The bird was too smart to allow itself to be caught so easily. It was perched well out of reach. The snakes could only leap about five feet into the air and it was roosting at least eight feet from the ground.

We were about a quarter of the way into the ruins now. Using the tip of my spear, we walked in single file with me in the lead. Moving slowly drew less attention, so we took our time to make our way through the marsh.

Chapter Thirty-Six

The closer we drew to the center of the ruined city, the fewer attacks I had to face. It almost seemed like the snakes were avoiding the deepest part of the swamp. It was eerily quiet when we finally reached a building that only had a few walls standing. The floor seemed stable enough, so we walked over to the edge to peer out into the gloom.

"I have a bad feeling about this," Sam said uneasily. I knew what he meant. The raven was still watching us expectantly. Its beak was open as if it was grinning and getting ready to laugh. No doubt, its amusement would be at my expense.

Examining the center of the ruins, I was pretty sure it had once housed a palace. The entire building was gone and nothing remained. If I hadn't been paying close attention, I might have been tricked into thinking that the ground was solid. Only the tiny ripples in the surface of the sludge gave away that it was a swamp.

The smell was particularly bad here. My olfactory senses had shut down in self-defense some time ago, but I couldn't quite ignore this stench. Sam's eyes were watering in protest. He squinted at the quagmire. "Are you certain that the piece of the object is somewhere in there? It does not seem like a very secure place to hide it."

"I'm pretty sure it's in there somewhere," I said with a mental groan. The thought of slogging around in the muck didn't fill me with joy. Snakes would be drawn to us in droves and we'd have a constant battle on our hands. I had no idea how we were going to find the object in the ooze. "I guess I'd better see how deep it is."

Leaning forward to insert my spear into the sludge, it didn't meet resistance as I'd expected. I lost my balance and fell headfirst into the quagmire. I made two mistakes when I landed. I opened my mouth to scream and I let go of my weapon. The bright scarlet light of the blade faded almost immediately as it sank down into the gloom. The ooze was so thick that I was effectively blinded.

Kicking my legs hard to propel myself upwards, I burst up onto the surface and coughed up the sludge that I'd accidentally swallowed. Several thoughts went through my head at once; I hoped I didn't catch some kind of bug from swallowing the crud, my favorite jacket might be ruined forever and how the hell was I going to get this crap out of my hair?

Sam gaped at me, then doubled over in laughter. He leaned against the wall for balance, pointing at me and giggling hysterically.

"Nice," I said with heavy sarcasm, moving my legs in the thick sludge so I could stay afloat. It wasn't as easy as treading water. "I didn't laugh at you when you fell into the hole." I'd kept my amusement to myself.

He managed to gain enough control to respond. "You should have seen your face when you realized you were going in." He mimicked my horror and resignation so well that I had to grin.

Reaching out, he offered me his hand, then alarm flitted over his face. I looked over my shoulder to see a gigantic ripple working its way outwards from the center of the swamp. I'd drifted a few yards away from safety and I instinctively knew that I wouldn't make it back in time to avoid whatever disaster was coming for me.

Turning to meet my best friend's eyes, there were a thousand things that I wanted to say to him, but I didn't have the time. Something huge erupted beneath me, launching me high into the air. Spinning head over heels, I saw a wide throat that led down into darkness and razor sharp teeth that were longer than I was. It was another snake, but this one was monstrous in size.

Reaching its peak, gravity took over and the

gargantuan began to fall backwards. My stomach flopped over as I free-fell towards its throat. I banged into its teeth and they sliced my legs open to the bone. Landing on its gigantic black tongue, I lay on my back, stunned and bleeding.

The mammoth sized snake was about to descend beneath the surface when Sam did something that was both heroic and stupid. He jumped in with me. Before I could scold him for his actions, the teeth closed tight and the beast swallowed. We were sent tumbling down its throat and into its stomach.

Landing in fluid that was waist high on me, I floundered to my feet. Gagging at the acidic stench, I didn't have anything in my stomach to bring up and dry heaved until I managed to regain control. My legs only burned in pain for a few seconds before the cuts healed.

"Are you crazy?" I said to my companion. It came out as a croak. My throat was too clogged to be able to yell at him like I wanted to. "What were you thinking?"

"I promised Nathan that I would protect you," he said simply as he climbed to his feet. "Besides, you would have done the same thing for me." That was true. I wouldn't have just stood there and watched while he'd been swallowed up by the behemoth.

Sam peered into the darkness, holding the steak knife in a white knuckled grip. I wished I hadn't dropped my weapon. As if reacting to that thought, crimson light blazed to life about fifty yards away. It didn't just illuminate the darkness, it also highlighted the fact that we weren't alone down here. Creatures stirred, drawn by the glow.

We slogged our way through the gut juice over to my dagger. Holding my breath, I bent down and became momentarily submerged again until I grasped hold of it. Wiping the noisome fluid off my face with my hand, I moved closer to Sam as the stomach dwellers came forward.

Thin, haggard and covered in sores, a hundred or so lesser demons closed in around us and stared at us dully. Their sackcloth had long since rotted away in the gastric juices that were even now eating away at my clothing and skin.

"It is a human," one of the females said in astonishment. She examined Sam and her lip curled. "And an imp. The most useless of all beings that resides in hell."

"He isn't useless," I said in Sam's defense. His shoulders sagged as they always did whenever someone belittled him. "He's my guide and my friend."

"Ooh, he is your friend," the hell spawn mocked and rolled her eyes. "I stand corrected. What are you doing here? Are you not aware that the city is cursed?"

"Obviously not," I retorted. "We came here to find a piece of metal about this big." I held up my palm to indicate the size. "Have any of you seen it?"

Their eyes flicked away from me furtively. One of

the demons had his hands behind his back. The others shuffled in front of him to hide him from my sight.

"No," the female spokesdemon said. "We have seen nothing new since we were swallowed by this creature two millennia ago."

I knew they were lying, but I let it go for now. I had a much more pressing question to ask, thanks to my innate curiosity. "Why was the city cursed? How did the swamp come to be?"

They exchanged looks, then she leaned in to whisper to me. "The Prince did something that displeased the Hellmaster. It is said that Satan cursed the city and stripped the Prince of his power and cast him back to the first realm. The ground turned to sludge and the snakes took up residence. Then the palace sank and this creature was placed here to ensure that no one would ever try to rebuild on this site."

"I guess another Prince must have risen and built a new city and a palace far away from here."

She shrugged in unconcern. "I would not know. We have been trapped here ever since that fateful day."

While she'd been talking, they'd subtly moved to surround us. Weapons began to appear in their hands. Most were daggers like mine, but others held short swords. "You don't want to attack me," I warned them.

"Why not?" Her expression had turned sly. "We are

tired of torturing the souls that were swallowed along with us. You two will offer us some much needed entertainment."

"We really won't," I replied and my dagger became an axe. "Haven't you figured out who I am yet?"

Staring at my weapon, she looked at me in wild hope. "Could it be?"

"Hellscourge?" someone whispered. It wasn't said in horror, but in profound hope.

"Gold of hair, green of eye," someone chanted.

"Bearing two opposing natures," another demon continued.

"She shall purge the nine realms of its leaders," a third intoned.

"Leaving devastation in her wake," a fourth recited.

Their spokesdemon finished the last line herself. "The Hellscourge shall bring death to any who incurs her wrath."

"That's right," I confirmed. "I've already killed two Princes."

Instead of fleeing in terror, she turned to Sam. "Is this true, imp?"

"It is," he replied with a nod. "I witnessed one of their deaths myself. She beheaded the first one and gutted the second." He said it as if he was proud of me.

"I know you have the object we're searching for," I said and pointed at the demon who was trying to hide it from me. "Just hand it over and no one needs to get hurt."

"You do not understand," their leader said and her weapon disappeared. "We will not fight you." She gestured for the demon who was holding the object to come forward. "We will gladly give you this trinket, on one condition."

I knew that making a bargain with a demon was a bad idea, but I felt compelled to ask anyway. "What condition?"

"We want you to kill us."

I blinked at her unexpected answer. "Why?"

"Because we are tired of living in this miserable existence," she said wearily. "There is no way out of this prison." She cast her hand around, indicating the stomach that we were trapped inside. "Death would be better than this." She said it bleakly and heads nodded in agreement. One by one, their weapons winked out of existence. The lesser demon opened his hand to reveal the piece of metal. About the size of my palm, it was tarnished silver and bore faint impressions that I couldn't make out.

Looking at Sam for his opinion, he nodded, but he seemed disturbed. "If I had been imprisoned here for two millennia, I would want to die as well," he told me.

"Fine," I said and reached out to pick up the object. I slipped it into my pocket, then motioned for them to line up. "I'll try to make your deaths painless."

Their hideous faces twisted in something close to joy as they complied. I swung my axe up and their spokesdemon leaned forward, offering me her neck. The blade sliced down and cut through her flesh with ease.

At first, it didn't bother me to end their lives. By the twentieth execution, I was starting to feel queasy. By the fiftieth, I wasn't sure that I could continue on with the mindless slaughter. When I was near the end, I had to force myself to swing the axe. As soon as the last one fell, I surveyed the long line of headless bodies and came close to bursting into tears. They had lined up and had begged to die, but I still felt like a mass murderer.

Sam folded me into his arms and stroked his hand down my filthy hair. "It was an act of mercy," he said gently. "You should not feel bad about ending their lives."

"I can't help it," I half-sobbed. "They just stood there like sheep and let me cut their heads off!" It was so un-demon like that I couldn't understand how they'd given up all hope. If I was trapped down here, I'd stop at nothing to free myself. Come to think of it, I *was* imprisoned down here now. We were in exactly the same position that they'd been in, but we didn't have anyone who could end our existence or our endless misery.

Chapter Thirty-Seven

Once I'd regained control of my emotions. Sam voiced the same question that I'd been asking myself. "How are we going to get out of here?" He peered around the cavernous stomach, futilely searching for a way out. If a way had existed, I was pretty sure the demons would have found it by now.

"I don't know. I guess I'll have to try to carve my way through its flesh." I didn't relish the idea, but I didn't know what else to do. This thing was at least a couple of thousand years old, which meant it was probably immortal. Then again, I was the scourge of hell. If I could kill demons, maybe I would be able to kill it as well.

We sloshed through the putrid gastric juices until we reached the stomach wall. Hefting my axe, I cut into the rubbery membrane. It took several tries before I perforated the lining. I felt the beast flinch when blood spurted over me. It added to the stains that already soaked my clothes.

"I think it felt that one," Sam said. He was keeping his distance from me to avoid the blood splatters. His guess was confirmed when I swung my axe again. The monster bellowed and the echo came all the way down to us. I chopped into it again and lost my balance when it surged into motion.

Sam reached for me and we clutched each other as the gigantic snake frantically swam around in dizzying patterns. Stopping, it heaved a few times. We looked at each other in horror when we realized what it was going to do. "This is going to be gross," I predicted, then the snake vomited.

Tumbling head over heels, we were swept back along its stomach and up through its throat. My legs had healed from the deep gashes, but I was torn open again as I swept between two of its teeth. We landed with a wet splat on solid ground, but we weren't alone. Souls by the thousands were ejected along with us. They'd been deeper within its digestive tract where we hadn't been able to see or hear them.

Screaming and wailing, the souls thrashed around, believing they were suffering from some new form of torment. The chains that had once bound them together had long ago disintegrated from the acid that had done an excellent job of staining our clothes.

I exchanged a relieved look with Sam that we'd been dumped beside the lake that had taken the palace's place. The massive maw of the snake began to close as it retreated into the swamp. Its scarlet eyes were narrowed in rage and pain as it slowly slid back beneath the sludge.

Still sitting on the crumbling wall as if it had been savoring our demise, the raven gave a frustrated caw at seeing us escape so soon. It took to wing and flapped off into the distance. It was no doubt speeding off to warn its master that we were still intact. I was pretty sure the Hellmaster wanted me alive, but he'd intended to punish me first. We'd only spent a short amount of time in the snake's gut, but it had been more than long enough for me.

The giant snake's much smaller offspring left us in peace this time as we slogged through the calf-deep sludge towards the outskirts of town. Maybe they knew that their gigantic overlord had been wounded and were now too afraid to attack us.

It hadn't escaped me that murdering the demons hadn't been necessary after all. They could have been vomited out with us, but it was too late now. I didn't know why I felt so bad about killing them. Maybe because they'd been so pathetically desperate to die.

Sam kept sending me sidelong looks that I couldn't quite interpret. "What?" I asked when I couldn't take it anymore.

"You look different."

"Different how?"

He cocked his head to the side and seemed reluctant to answer me. "I think your skin is darker."

Looking down at my hands, I snorted out a laugh. "I'm completely covered in crud. Of course my skin is darker."

"It is not just your skin that is different," he said even more reluctantly. "You have bumps on your forehead."

My hand flew to my forehead in horror. Sure enough, two lumps were beginning to form. I was almost afraid to ask, but I forced the words out. "Does anything else about me look different?"

"Your eyes are changing color."

"They're turning red, aren't they?" I asked with foreboding. He nodded and it was all I could do not to cry.

Wishing I'd never fled from Denver and ended up in New York to be dragged into this destiny, I mentally called on the nightmares. They appeared moments later and rapidly galloped towards us. Stopping a few yards away, they both turned their heads to survey us. Their nostrils flared in apparent disgust. "I know we stink," I said dismally. "There's no need to make an issue of it."

Pawing at the ground soundlessly, they tossed their manes in agitation, but allowed us to climb into the carriage. I sank down onto the cushioned seat in gratitude. Something fluttered inside my stomach and I went stock still. Sam had also collapsed onto his seat in exhaustion. His eyes were closed, so I took a moment to lift up my jacket and shirt. The scar had thickened and the tendrils had lengthened. They were moving as if a gentle wind was blowing them.

Feeling ill, I dropped my clothes to cover the hideous sight and closed my eyes as well. We lurched into motion and I fell asleep to the clatter of the wheels over the hard ground.

It felt like only moments had passed before I was standing in front of the legion inside my mind. "What's happening to me?" I said to Morax straight away.

He looked tired, but not as exhausted as I felt. "We have been discussing this," he said, indicating the other Demon Lords. "We believe your body is beginning to change because of the toxin that the Wraith Warrior infected you with."

"It's turning me into one of you, isn't it?" I said in dread.

He inclined his head in agreement. "So it would seem." They weren't particularly happy about it. The more like them I became, the less likely it was that I would find a way to evict them from my mind.

With a nod of thanks, I trudged over to Heather's house. She threw the door open and pulled me inside before I could knock. "Are you all right?" she asked. I was clean in my dream and she didn't hesitate to give me a hug.

"I'm fine," I replied. That might be true physically, but I was a wreck mentally. Sy was sitting on the floor in the living room, sketching out some new runes. He looked up and nodded in acknowledgement that I was there. "I want to thank you both for keeping me sane when I was in the rat tunnels," I said.

"That's okay," Heather replied. "We all know how important it is for you to keep your mind intact." She might not interact with the legion, but she knew as well as they did that I was their only key to eventual freedom.

Chapter Thirty-Eight

Sam woke me by urgently shaking my shoulder. "You need to wake up," he said.

His tone had me sitting up from my slump. "What's wrong?" I looked around to see we were still in the carriage.

"We are nearing the gate."

"Already? That was quick."

"Not really. It took us nearly two days to get here."

I looked at him blankly. My dream had broken up fairly quickly and I remembered nothing after that. "Was I asleep the whole time?"

"Yes. I thought it was best to let you get your rest."

"Thanks." I didn't feel rested. I felt groggy and out of sorts.

"You should look out the window. I think we may have a slight problem with getting back into the shadowlands."

Disturbed by his ominous tone, I pushed the window up and looked outside. The tall black wall that penned in the demons like unholy cattle was visible ahead. I could see the gate waiting for us and it wasn't alone. A full regiment of a thousand soldiers was arrayed before it.

"This is not good," I agreed. "If we manage to break through them, we can't risk them following us." That had happened the last time and I'd ended up with a hundred extra troops to add to my legion. I didn't know how the regiment had found this particular entrance, then I realized that the raven had to be responsible. It had relayed everything to its master and he'd sent these lackeys to intercept us.

"I do not think you can stop them from following us into the shadowlands."

"There has to be a way," I said, thinking fast. I snapped my fingers when I remembered something. "The gate said it moves to wherever its needed. What if we choose a different spot on the wall and see if it will shift to us?"

Sam's mouth dropped open. "You can be truly brilliant sometimes."

"Thanks," I said wryly. I didn't kid myself that I was a genius, but even I had my moments.

Reacting to my thoughts, the nightmares veered away from the regiment. A Demon Lord and the captain in charge of the soldiers shouted orders. They took off after us at a run, but we rapidly left them in our dust.

Picking a spot about a mile away from where the gate had originally been, I silently asked the hellhorses to stop. Sticking my head out the window again, I crossed my fingers that this was going to work. "Gate! I need you!"

A section of the wall shimmered and the gate appeared, complete with its pet gargoyles. A face formed in the wrought iron. His dismal expression and decorations of humans performing the arts told me it was the same gate that we'd used to enter this realm. "There is no need to shout," he said sourly. "My hearing is exceptional."

"Sorry," I said. "Would you mind opening for us?"

He heaved a put-upon sigh. "I suppose I must." A groaning sound commenced and a crack appeared down the middle of the gate. It slowly began to swing open and Sam tugged on my sleeve.

"We have another problem," he said.

"The soldiers can't have caught up to us yet," I replied and turned to see how close they were. As I'd guessed, they were still distant. Hearing a hollow howl from behind us, the hairs on the back of my neck rose. I scrambled across the carriage and squeezed in beside Sam. A pack of hellhounds was closing in on us fast. Their crimson eyes gleamed in bloodlust as their feet noiselessly covered the ground.

Diving over to the window, I stuck my head out. "Hurry!" I shouted at the gate.

"I cannot move any faster," he said, looking at me glumly.

Shifting restlessly, the nightmares rolled their eyes. They were fearsome in their own right, but neither of them wanted to take on a pack of six hellhounds. The moment there was enough room for the carriage to squeeze through, they took off at a gallop.

"Don't let the hellhounds through!" I ordered the gate.

"It is already too late to prevent them from leaving," he lamented as he began to swing shut. The dogs managed to race through the opening, but the regiment of soldiers had been locked in hell. Nearly nipping at our heels, I could almost smell the hounds' breath as they sprinted after us. The hellhorses galloped as fast as they could, widening the gap between us and our pursuers. Sam and I watched through the back window as the demonic dogs fell further and further behind.

Knowing we had to be close to the portal that would take us home, we turned around just as the carriage disappeared. One of the nightmares appeared beneath us before we could fall to the ground. Riding bareback now, Sam held onto the horse's mane and I gripped him tightly around the waist. I risked a look back to see the hellhounds silently pounding after us.

Entering the narrow alleyway, we braced ourselves a moment before the horse skidded to a stop and bucked us off. As always, Nathan was there to catch me. Leo was there to save Sam from splattering on the road. Brie was a no-show this time.

"I have you," Nathan said, drinking in the sight of me. Staring into his beautiful eyes, I was on the verge of becoming lost in their depths.

Remembering the danger that had followed us, I turned to see the nightmare spin around. It galloped off, disappearing from sight. Seconds later, I saw the pack of hellhounds sprinting through the darkness. Skidding to a stop just like the nightmare had, the alpha dog's head emerged from the portal. Crimson eyes glowed eerily in the dark as its shadowy head appeared to be sticking out of the rock wall.

"Yikes!" Leo exclaimed and stumbled back a step, dragging Sam with him. The hound bared its fangs in disappointment that I was out of its reach. Instead of attacking me, it slowly drew back before turning away and fading from sight.

Letting out a breath I didn't realize I'd been holding, I looked up at Nathan. He smiled in relief that I was intact and it took everything I had not to mash my lips against his. His eyes dropped to my mouth as if he'd read my mind.

"I am so glad that you are back," he said. "You were gone for so long that we were beginning to worry."

By my count, we'd been gone for nearly five days. Nathan put me down and I surreptitiously checked my forehead. Relief swept through me when I didn't find any suspicious lumps. I checked my hands, but they were too dirty to see if my skin was a different color. "How long were we gone?" I asked.

"Twelve days."

Alarmed to hear that, I felt my pocket for my cell phone then remembered that I'd left it in my room. "Zach will be wondering where I am." His lips tightened at the mention of my boyfriend.

"Do not worry," Leo said. "I came to the rescue. I heard your cell phone make a noise and checked it to see that there was a message from your beau." I must have left it on vibrate rather than silent. I made a face at the nickname they'd all decided to call him. It was ridiculously archaic and they used it just to annoy me. "I worked out how to use the device and sent him a message," he added.

"What did you say to him?" I couldn't hide my trepidation. Leo was the most progressive of my friends, but he didn't know much about how human relationships worked.

"I told him you were feeling ill and that you would contact him when you felt better."

I reached over and gave him a hug. "Thanks, Leo. You're the best."

"Did you locate the object?" Nathan asked.

"Yeah." I dug it out of my pocket and handed it to him.

Closing his hand around it, he slipped it into his own pocket. "We should get back to our base," he decided. "You look like you could use some rest." I didn't bother to tell him that I'd slept for two days straight. The rest I had in hell wasn't the same as sleeping in my own dimension. I felt drained of energy and weary to my very bones.

Chapter Thirty-Nine

Sophia smiled widely when she noticed that we'd appeared next to the table, but Brie merely scowled. The clairvoyant stood and drew both Sam and me into a hug. She winced at the smell that wafted off us. I could apparently repair rips and tears in hell, but I couldn't make dirt disappear. "You should take a shower," she suggested. "I will soak your clothes overnight and see if I can rid them of that awful odor."

"Thanks, Sophia," I said with genuine gratitude. Once again, she was stepping up to take on the role of my foster mother.

We trudged upstairs and I motioned for Sam to shower first. He took longer than usual, but I knew I would be in the bathroom for a lot longer than him. I stripped off in preparation and pulled on a robe.

A soft knock came at the door and I knew who it was even before I opened it. Nathan stood in the doorway. Knowing it would be dangerous for us to be alone behind a closed door, he didn't enter the room. "Did you sustain any injuries while you were in hell?"

"A few," I admitted. I held up a hand and stepped back out of his reach when he instinctively took a step towards me. "I'm fine now. The legion healed me." My hand went to the scar on my abdomen. I could almost feel the rot spreading through me. The wound wasn't bleeding, but it definitely wasn't completely healed.

"Are you in pain?" he asked me softly.

"No. Not yet."

We both knew that wouldn't last. The Wraith Warrior had ensured that I was doomed no matter which dimension I was in. If I stayed on Earth, my insides would putrefy. If I spent too long in hell, I would take on the physical shape of a demon. I was in a lose-lose situation.

"What are you two doing?" Brie asked suspiciously from behind Nathan. He turned to show her that we weren't even touching.

"We're having a civil conversation," I said with exaggerated patience. "That's a skill you haven't mastered yet, but don't worry, you might eventually get the hang of it in another century or two."

Sam shut off the shower just in time to overhear my stinging barb. A chuckle sounded inside the bathroom and Brie cut a glare in his direction.

"Hagith and Orifiel have asked to be updated with your progress. I will retrieve them while you have your shower." She sent me a frown that wasn't particularly scary since she had the young and angelic face of a teenager. "We will be back shortly. Do not keep us waiting."

She disappeared and Nathan flicked me a look. "When shall I advise Sophia to have tea ready for you? Will twenty minutes suffice?"

"You'd better make it thirty," I said with a grin. He knew me well. Brie's order for me to hurry had pretty well guaranteed that I would take my time. Besides, I had a lot of crud to scrape off my skin, not to mention to wash out of my hair.

Sam emerged from the bathroom while I was watching my guardian walk away. Nathan sent me a sardonic look over his shoulder, as if he knew I was admiring the view. Pushing aside my hopeless longing for him, I waited for Sam to reach me before I spoke. "We should probably keep the fact that I'm turning into a demon to ourselves," I whispered.

If Hag and Orifice found out about this, our tentative alliance with them would be shattered. I already had enough enemies to deal with and I didn't want to add any more to the list. I wasn't sure how my friends would react if they knew. It was best to remain silent about it.

He nodded in agreement. "I had the same thought. They will probably try to question me while you are in the shower. I believe I will stay up here and watch television until you are ready to join them."

Seeing the way he kept glancing towards the living room just across the hall, I narrowed my eyes. "You're a TV junkie and you're dying for your next fix."

His gaze slid away from mine and he assumed an innocent expression. "I do not know what you are talking about."

"The first step to conquering an addiction is to admit that you have one," I said solemnly.

"I am not addicted," he insisted. "I can stop watching it whenever I please."

"Sure you can," I said with a grin and stepped around him. "By the way, that's what all junkies say about their addictions."

Stepping into the bathroom, I heard his rapid footsteps enter the living room. The TV came on even before I locked the door. Hanging my robe on a hook, I switched on the shower. It was impossible not to see the disturbing scar on my stomach as I did my best to wash away the accumulation of grime. Something stirred when I rubbed the washcloth over the thick black ridge. I had to press my lips together to hold in a moan of dread. I wasn't sure if there was something alive in there, or if it was just my internal organs reacting to the infection.

It took even longer than I'd anticipated before I finally managed to get all of the dried sludge out of my hair. It was closer to forty minutes than thirty when I shut the water off. Drying myself off, I dressed in jeans and a hoodie, then went to retrieve Sam. He didn't even notice me standing in the doorway. His eyes were glued to the screen as he watched whatever had captured his attention. I hated to drag him away, but I needed his moral support for the grilling that I was about to receive. "Are you coming downstairs?" I asked.

Tearing his eyes away from the screen, he heaved himself to his feet. "I have a lot of programs to catch up on," he said, "but I will watch them while you sleep."

"You recorded them while we were gone?" I asked incredulously.

His nod was sheepish. "It is actually quite easy to set the device to record automatically." Sophia might not watch television very often, but she'd bought the required gadgets to be able to watch and record shows.

"I'm going to crash as soon as the inquisition is over," I said as we headed down the stairs. "I'll probably be out for hours." Maybe I'd sleep for two full days just like I had in hell. I felt almost weary enough to fall into a coma.

Chapter Forty

Wintry silence met us when we stepped into the front room. Hagith and Orifiel were standing side by side stiffly. Neither deigned to look in our direction until after we'd taken our seats. "I am sure you delighted in keeping us waiting for as long as possible," Hagith said with her usual sneer. "It is proof of just how childish you truly are."

I looked her directly in the eye and stared at her without responding. The silence grew even more uncomfortable until Sophia shifted restlessly. "Violet? Are you going to share what happened to you in the seventh realm with us?"

"Sure. Just as soon as Hagith apologizes to me."

The blond angel's mouth dropped open and Orifiel looked aghast. "I will do no such thing!" she declared. "Briathos advised you that we would be here shortly.

You should have had the decency to be ready for when we arrived."

"Have you ever been swallowed by a gigantic hellsnake?" I asked.

She was taken aback by my conversational tone. "No."

"Well, Sam and I have and it did some pretty disgusting things to our hair and skin."

"Then there was the sludge from the swamp," Sam added and shuddered. "That stench will linger for a while."

Leo was struggling hard to control himself and lost. Heads whipped towards him when he sniggered. Nathan was doing a better job of containing his amusement. He sat with his arms crossed, waiting patiently. A tiny smile played around his perfect mouth.

Sophia knew I wasn't going to budge until I got what I wanted. "Hagith, please apologize to Violet and Samuel. It appears that they have gone through some very trying ordeals. I am sure she will be happy to tell us the full story once you have appeased her."

Hagith struggled not to vent her frustration. Orifiel put a hand on her shoulder and gave her a meaningful look. Brie rolled her eyes at us all. "Please just apologize so we can all get on with our mission," she suggested. She was far more polite to the angels than she'd ever been to me.

Her back went even stiffer as Hagith mumbled something that sounded vaguely like an apology. I was going to ask her to repeat it, but Nathan caught my eye and shook his head in warning.

"Fine," I said with a huff. "This is what happened." With Sam's help, I relayed the story about how we'd infiltrated the prince's palace. I told them that I'd tortured him for information about where he'd put the object. We carefully avoided any reference to my skin changing color or the horns that had seemed to be growing on my forehead. I also didn't mention my questions about the angel souls that had been collected and what their purpose was. That was just between Sophia and me. Since I hadn't learned anything, there was no point bringing it up anyway.

"When we returned to the gate, we found an entire regiment of demons waiting for us," I finished up. "I went with a hunch and asked the nightmares to veer away. After a mile or so, they stopped and I called out for the hellgate. Just as I'd hoped, it moved to our location. We were able to leave without taking the entire regiment through with us."

"A pack of hellhounds followed us into the shadowlands, though," Sam added. "They almost came through the portal after us." The Demon Lord, or his captain, would have had to challenge the gate and survive the nine trials in order for them to follow us. Even then, they'd only be able to take five lackeys with them. But I was pretty sure I was the only one who could use the shortcuts to Earth. Defeating the master gate had to be the reason why I was able to find the portals.

"They would not have survived for long," Orifiel said. "Creatures that were created in hell cannot exist in this realm."

That explained why the hounds had turned tail and had slunk off rather than leaving the portal and attacking us when they'd had the chance. The undead raven was different. It had been born here and had been taken through to hell by the Hellmaster to be his eyes and ears.

"You have killed two of the Demon Princes," Hagith said. "You have also found three pieces of this object of power."

I could have said something snarky about her ability to state the obvious, but Sam elbowed me in the side before the words could escape. "Yep," I said instead. "That about sums it up."

"May we see the pieces?" She directed the question to Sophia, who nodded and pushed her chair back and stood. She took the stairs to the second floor and came back with a metal box. Putting it on the table in front of Brie, she waited for the teen to unlock it with a spell. Flipping the lid open, she revealed two tarnished silver metal pieces.

Hagith took them out and put them on the table. Nathan added the latest piece that I'd found beside them. The edges were jagged and reminded me of a jigsaw puzzle. Hagith moved them around, trying to fit them together, but none of the pieces fit. "Can anyone make out what these images are?" she asked.

They were so faint that they were barely noticeable.

We all shook our heads and I lifted my arm that held the crimson bracelet and pulled the sleeve back. "They look a lot like the images that keep appearing on my bracelet." I noticed that more images had appeared after I'd killed the second prince.

Hagith and Orifiel stared at me in horror that was mixed with a tinge of fear. "Why did you not tell us about this sooner?" Hag said in a strangled tone and flicked a look at Brie. I'd forgotten that they hadn't seen the color of my bracelet. It should have been golden in color. Instead, it was as crimson as my dagger. Sam's was a dingy gray color, presumably because he was an imp.

"I did not think it was important," she said in self-defense. I'd tried to hide this development from them, but they'd obviously noticed the gradual change. Nathan had been aware of it. He'd been trying to help me keep this a secret.

"In the future, you will advise us of anything that happens in relation to Violet, no matter how small you believe it may be." Her tone was scathing. Exchanging a glance, she and her sidekick disappeared. Brie sent me a sullen look, clearly blaming me for her public reprimand. I had no idea which angelic order our allies came from, but they were clearly higher in the hierarchy than the rest of our gang.

Sophia placed the metal pieces back into the box and Brie locked it again. They were apparently important to the Hellmaster, but I still didn't know what they were, or what their purpose was. It was all part of the puzzle I'd have to solve in my quest to stop the demon apocalypse from occurring.

My mission had become even more urgent with the changes that were happening to my body. I still had six more princes to eradicate and six more pieces of the object to find. I would also have to deal with the Hellmaster at some stage.

Each time I was hell bound, I faced the danger that I would become the very thing that I was supposed to be fighting. All signs were indicating that I would eventually turn into a demon. I was in a race against time and I had no control over when I'd find the next portal to hell. I had to trust that Fate would guide me and that she wouldn't abandon me to face my destiny alone.

Printed in Great Britain
by Amazon